Nor Heard the Clock Strike

Nor Heard the Clock Strike

Alastair Christie-Johnston

The Shetland Times Ltd.
Lerwick
2004

Nor Heard the Clock Strike

ISBN 1 904746 04 7

First published by The Shetland Times Ltd., 2004.

British Library Cataloguing-in-Publication Data
A catalogue record for this book is available from the British Library.

Printed and published by
The Shetland Times Ltd.,
Gremista, Lerwick,
Shetland ZE1 0PX, UK.

Contents

For Adaline

Preface

As any Shetlander will readily tell you, Bruntisdale does not exist. It is a figment of my imagination. In creating it, however, I have tried to give some authenticity to the story by using family names and place names that are recognisably of Shetland origin. Any resemblance to persons living or dead is entirely coincidental.

I was born in Shetland and *did* live there for a period in 1975. My wife is also a Shetlander. We now live in Tasmania, Australia.

Some of the events I describe, such as the sheep shearing, are authentic memories of very happy occasions. Many others are pure fiction. Places and business names in Lerwick are authentic. The story of the shipwrecked boy was told to me by the late Jimmy Isbister of Foula in more or less the form given. I have heard similar versions from others also and believe it is already in print. I make no apology for repeating it here. Such stories are very much a part of the fabric of Shetland life.

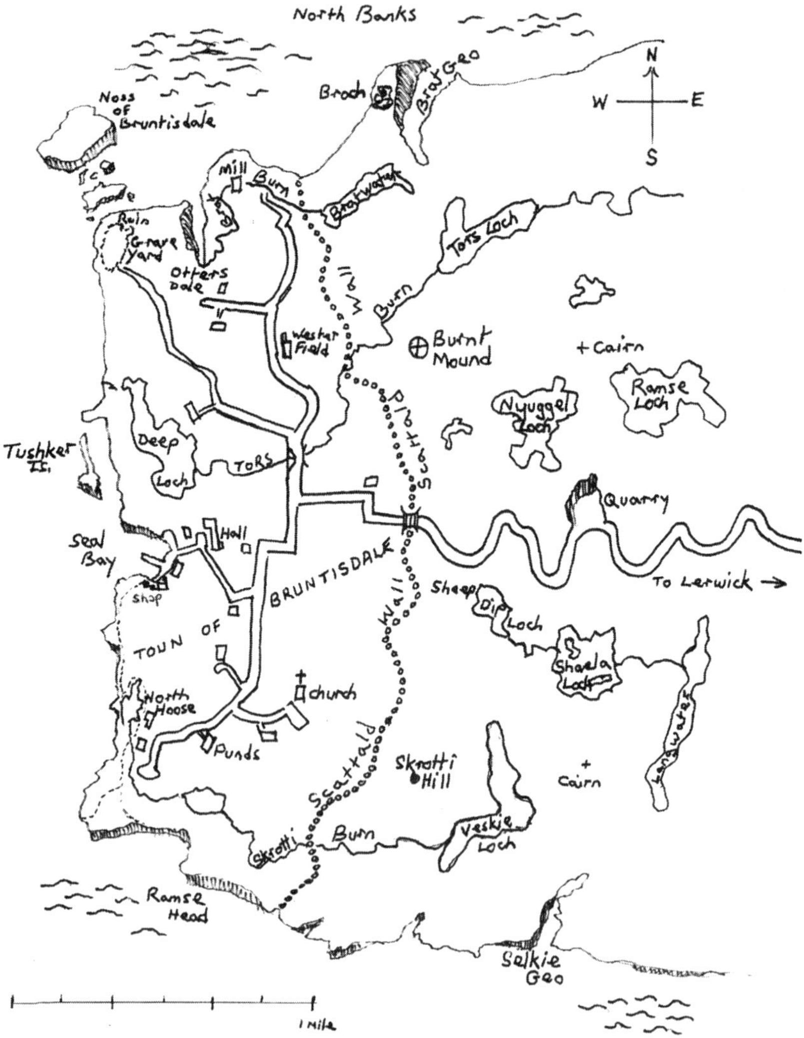
North Banks
Noss of Bruntisdale
Broch
Brat Geo
N
W
E
S
Mill
Burn
Ruin
Grave Yard
Otters Dale
Tors Loch
Wall
Burn
Wester Field
Burnt Mound
+ Cairn
Ramse Loch
Nyuggel Loch
Deep Loch
TORS
Tushker Is.
Quarry
Seal Bay
Hall
Shop
BRUNTISDALE
TOUN OF
To Lerwick →
Sheep Dip Loch
Wall
church
North Hoose
Punds
Scattald
Skrotti Hill
Cairn
Skrotti Burn
Veskie Loch
Ramse Head
Selkie Geo
1 Mile

Chapter One

The road seemed to go on forever, winding through the hills. Interminable miles of sameness. Endless barren moorland dotted with lochs. No trees, of course. This was Shetland.

Here and there the road skirted a loch. In summer you could glimpse waterlilies in the shallow peaty water. If you were lucky you might see a breeding pair of red-throated divers. In winter, flocks of whooper swans congregated on the deeper lochs – the ones that had not frozen over. Once I saw a weasel dancing in the snow. White on white. A mesmerising undulation. The memory of it haunts me still.

Of course the hills and lochs petered out eventually. Nothing is really forever. One last loch. One last hill. And then the pewter sea fading away to the horizon and pewter sky. Except on rare sunny days when everything seemed to stretch a little further, the way a smile stretches a face. On sunnier days the moor smiled a little too, folding its wrinkles into subtle tones like the shades of wool on a colour card for Shetland knitwear – moorit, bracken, lichen, heather. All slashed through with the Shetland black of the peat banks. On those better days the sky might be duck-egg blue and the sea silver scaled like a mackerel.

Here, where the barrenness of the scattald met the green of the outfields, a high freestone wall formed the demarcation line. A grid kept the hill sheep out. On still nights you might hear a harsh rattle, like stones shaken in a tin, and know a car was westering home through the rusty barrier. In the lee of the wall the hill sheep congregated to find shade or shelter, sometimes spilling across the road with lambs skittering behind them. It was a place for cautious driving in a hill fog or a night of lashing rain.

Below the grid the first dwellings could be seen dotted amongst the neat rigs of corn and potatoes. Two-storeyed whitewashed croft houses, with long, low barns at their gables. Peat smoke drifting over tarred felt roofs. This mile or so of patchwork greens and browns between the scattald wall and the sea was known as the 'toun'. North and south the land rose to cliffs, but west, below the grid, the sea gentled into a bay to form a harbour of sorts. I had reached my destination, the village of Bruntisdale, though there was little enough to mark it as a village. Perhaps twenty-five houses in all. Less than ten in the vicinity of what might be termed the centre.

The black line of the road zig-zagged its way down to the centre of the village, passing, in a series of right angles, from one croft to the next. For centuries (so it was said), this was the way the cows had come home. First a hoof-beaten path, then a rutted track; next a gravelled, pot-holed lane, and finally a narrow, tarred road with passing places.

Beside the pierhouse, which was an imposing stone building of three storeys, there was a shop-cum-post office with a dwelling attached – a series of unimaginative add-ons that had clearly never been thwarted by officialdom in the guise of 'town planning' or 'building inspector'. This was where the road ended, spreading out in a shiny expanse of tar that shaped to the beach-head and pier. Old Bobby reckoned the county engineer had miscalculated on the required quantity of tarmacadam, so the roadmen just kept spreading it till it was all used up.

"You could land a bloody jumbo jet at the pierhouse if you had a mind to," he'd reckoned.

On the day of my arrival, I drove my car into the middle of that tarred expanse, unsure whether to park up by the pierhouse and shop or down at the pierhead. There were no lines to designate anything for the indecisive. A pod of whales could have beached here and caused no disruption to a village fair, supposing such a conjunction should occur.

A man was sitting on a bench outside the pierhouse. He took up a pair of binoculars and focussed them on me, shifting his gaze to the sea beyond, when he found me staring back. I was to learn, in time, this was Old Bobby. He spent the greater part of his days on that bench, scanning the horizon as though waiting for his ship to come in. He wore two fisherman's jerseys, one over the other, pulling his head down into the roll collars when he sighted a stranger, rather like a snail retreating into its shell when a shadow fell across it.

It took a lashing gale to drive Old Bobby indoors. At such times he took up station by the window of the pierhouse, where he commanded the same view. He was 'Old Bobby' to differentiate him from 'Young Bobby', who was no relation.

It seemed to be a feature of Bruntisdale that no-one went by their proper name. You were either designated by your place of abode – like 'Elsie the Loch' or 'Charlie Burnside', or by some eccentricity or physical feature – 'Danny Sheltie' (because he bred ponies); 'Maisie Hirple' (because she limped). With half a dozen Dannys and as many Charlies and Bobbys, there was never any risk of confusing one with another when each was so well defined.

Old Bobby, having pulled his head in as it were, ignored me. I left the vehicle and walked up to him. He didn't look the type to indulge in the usual meaningless chit-chat. The 'fine-weather-for-the-time-of-year' or 'how's-your-father?' brigade.

I came straight to the point.

"Car okay there, is it?"

"Looks okay to me." He smiled a little. Nothing to take liberties with, just a brief crinkling around the eyes, like a zephyr breeze on a calm pond, then back to reflecting nothing in particular.

He was looking past me, as if he might still be mildly embarrassed by having been caught out studying me through the binoculars. There was a shiftiness about him as he pulled his cap down a trifle more to shade his eyes. There was no knowing their colour. I'd have guessed he was about 75 though he might as easily be 95.

Shetlanders are like that. You can never be sure how old they are. When you are wondering if they are old enough to have seen service in the First World War they tell you they fought in the Boer War. They might quit work in their late 60s and spend the next 20 or 30 years watching the world go by, scarcely aging in the process.

They are good keepers, like the potatoes they store for winter under sacks in their barns, or the mutton and fish they soak in brine then hang at the gable-end to dry. Old Bobby might well have been salted and dried on his bench for all I knew, though in his case it would have been a cyclical process – the weather being what it was.

I left him to his daydreaming while I headed for the post office. I had no doubt he could furnish me with the information I sought, but I had a perverse desire to leave him with his curiosity unsated. If he were a cat it would kill him.

The post office had a bell. It allowed Peerie Jessie to get on with baking scones, or the washing and ironing, or whatever took her fancy between infrequent customers. She came through from the back room, wiping her hands on her apron. A buxom woman with wispy grey hair falling about her face. A few kirbigrips would not have gone astray. She had a cherry complexion, though whether from recent exertion or natural disposition, I couldn't tell. There was certainly a sort of windswept look about her, as though she had been buffeted by one gale too many in this land of gales. She wore wire-rimmed glasses well forward on her nose, giving me a green-eyed appraisal over the top of them. There was a firmness about her mouth that I translated into 'mind your step with this one'. Except I should have known better than to pre-judge in this way. First impressions are frequently misleading.

I would get to know Peerie Jessie better than anyone in the village, but for now she gave me a frosty reception and through it I totally misread her. It was clear I had interrupted something important, or more probably a tedious chore she was keen to be done with.

"What do you want?"

A touch of asperity there. Not exactly the warm welcome promised by the tourist brochures. I glanced round the shop, as if not knowing what I wanted. As I mentioned, it was more than a post office. I could see if I were a customer I need not bother being choosy. There was a take-it-or-leave-it selection of goods, by which I mean, if you wanted bread you better be happy with sliced white. Breakfast cereal meant cornflakes, and so on.

For the time being I'd settle for a pint of milk as I had most other essentials in the car. But first things first.

"I'm Stuart Graham. I've booked a place called 'Westerfield' for a month. I was told I'd get the key here."

"That's right enough," Peerie Jessie said, as though someone might have had the temerity to suggest otherwise.

She took a large key from a shelf behind her and handed it to me. The wooden tag was roughly poker-worked 'WESTERFIELD'.

"You go left at the fork a quarter mile back. North Road it's called. Westerfield is another mile and a half on your right. The name's on the gate. The key opens the front door. You'll find all the other keys and an information card on the kitchen table. I'm Peerie Jessie, by the way."

That seemed to be that. I thanked her and turned to leave.

"If you need any shopping we're open till seven."

Was that a belated olive branch?

"Oh yes," I remembered, "as a matter of fact I need some milk."

I was surprised to discover it came in a plastic bag. I had imagined collecting it in a billycan from a dairy, but then I supposed it was many years since the cows had wandered down the winding hill road to be milked in Bruntisdale. It was 1975 after all.

The square plastic bag was a novelty, none the less. A whole crateful stood on the counter like so many bags of frozen peas. I wondered how, in the name of creation, one was meant to cope with the thing. Perhaps a pin through the corner and a squeeze. Much like milking a cow. Surely not.

I found the house easily enough, wondering what sort of logic had put Westerfield on the North Road. It faced west so I supposed that might be reason enough. In such a featureless landscape it might be useful to have some compass points of reference.

It was a typical whitewashed croft house complete with barn and byre. The front door opened into a tiny porch from which a second door connected to a dark entrance passage. To the left was a low-ceilinged parlour. An open grate in the gable wall had a peat fire set ready to light. Matches on the mantelpiece.

Two chairs and matching sofa upholstered in brown velveteen were too large for the room and looked as if the springs might have sprung. A single low window in the two-foot-thick stone wall looked across the road to the open sea. Nice view. No window to the back.

The room opposite was of similar size with the same deep-set window. A second single-paned window in the gable gave added light and a view of the hills I had come through. This room was altogether more inviting with an oil-fired Rayburn stove that promised to provide a nice stuffy atmosphere on cold nights.

There was a six-by-four deal table, scrubbed white and covered in a blue checked oilcloth. It was surrounded by four padded upright chairs. A very battered armchair with a rug over it stood before the stove.

A pine dresser on the inside wall facing the Rayburn was stacked with Cornishware crockery. The walls were papered with cheery bud roses on a cream trellis background while the linoleum had a criss-cross pattern superimposed with waves and shells. It was a bit giddy-making if studied too closely.

I had heard tell of a Shetland woman knitting a Fair Isle jumper in the pattern of her linoleum. Judging by some of the garments I had seen in the streets of Lerwick that morning I was not surprised. There seemed to be no limit to the ingenuity of the women, especially when knitting for their own menfolk. It was apparently a matter of pride to try and outdo your neighbour in this regard.

From the front door a steep stair with no turning led to two low, coom-ceilinged bedrooms. I quickly chose the one over the kitchen, knowing the Rayburn would provide warmth through the floor. A trial bounce on the double bed was reassuring. Firm mattress, comfy feather quilt.

I had already decided to make the kitchen my base and dispense with the dreary parlour. Off the kitchen and under the angle of the stairs was a tiny scullery with a sink and plug-in stovette on a bench. A small refrigerator half blocked the open door, making the whole arrangement extremely cramped. I contemplated moving the fridge to make more space but there didn't appear to be anywhere to move it to – unless I put it in the middle of the floor.

I moved the kitchen table to under the front window where I would get maximum light. Not that I especially needed extra light, but the view was inspiring. Inspiration was meat and drink to me. I was a writer. I fetched my typewriter from the car and set it up on the table to prove the point. And yet, I should be honest, I was not so much a writer as a wannabe. This was the whole purpose of the exercise. But I will come to that in due course. The first thing was to sort myself out and make a cup of tea.

The information card Peerie Jessie had mentioned explained, amongst other things, that the weird looking plastic jug on the dresser was for the milk. You put the bag in then snipped off the corner with scissors and hey presto. I didn't much like the idea and was pleased to find a proper earthenware jug I could empty the bag into. Might as well start as I meant to go on.

I found the electric jug and where to turn the power on. That took care of the tea. While it was brewing, I lit the Rayburn. A quick shuftie at the information card, a couple of knobs and a pilot light did the trick. It would be good to warm the place up. It felt a bit damp and musty.

None of the windows opened but it was easy to create a through draught by leaving all the doors open. Oh, yes, I forgot to mention, there was a back door. It opened out of the kitchen corner next to the scullery and connected with a low passage that led to a concrete floored bathroom – enormous cast iron bath, water closet and hand basin surrounded by grey unpainted fibro walls. Obviously a post-war add-on and none too salubrious at that. It was anyone's guess what earlier occupants did for ablutions and the call of nature. Best not to enquire I decided.

Beyond the bathroom yet another door connected with the byre and eventually a back yard overgrown with dockens and nettles and goodness knows what else. Peats were stacked in one of the byre stalls. It was all clean enough. It would have been another story in the early days. The cows were permanently wintered in byres like this, along with the hens, the smell permeating to every corner of the house. One wore wellington boots to wade through the mire at milking time. I should thank God for small mercies – even if they were in plastic bags.

The tea was good. I sat at my kitchen window and took in the view. A couple of crofts, a glimpse of loch and beyond it the sea shining, half a mile away. The sun was occasionally blinking out of leaden clouds. I checked my watch. Three o'clock. It would still be light at ten-thirty as this was the last week in May. The best was yet to come. Shetlanders refer to the summer twilight as the simmer dim. In midsummer it is a permanent feature of the night sky. Sunset becomes sunrise with no discernible moment of transition.

My view west across the sea promised me some spectacular skies. I would be able to work at all hours, whenever the mood took me. At other times there would be long walks by shore and cliff. Fishing in the hill lochs. Perhaps I would hire a dinghy. Better still, buy one, and explore the caves. Already I could feel the spellbinding magic of the place beginning to seep into my bones. Or perhaps it was just that I needed that cup of tea more than I realised.

I unpacked the car. It was loaded to the gunnels with all manner of 'essential provisions'. You would have thought I was headed for Antarctica with Shackleton.

"It's the back of beyond," Clare had said. "You can't expect the village store to have any of the luxuries you are accustomed to pampering yourself with."

I had to admit she was right there. My cursory glance round the shelves of Peerie Jessie's shop had revealed a depressing lack of everything I considered essential to a well-stocked pantry.

Clare was my elder sister. If anyone knew my whims, she did. I had a younger sister, Anne, but we were never close. She took up with a theatrical freak in her teens and by all accounts spent most of her life backstage painting scenery. I hadn't seen her in years.

Clare and I stayed on at the manor house after father died. Mother had left us in Majorca in the summer of 1948 when I was seven. She had been smitten by a Hungarian count with a monocle and a fat bank balance. Not that my father was short of money, he was simply less inclined to part with it. When I grew up, I came to realise my mother had in all probability been attracted as much by the count's flamboyant lifestyle as his money. Like my younger sister, mother had a penchant for theatre.

There was certainly a distinct lack of theatre in my father. He was the epitome of a Scottish laird. Staid, dour, unimaginative; canny in the worst sense, and infuriatingly obstinate. On reflection, I can't imagine what possessed him to agree to a holiday in Majorca in the first place. It was not as if anyone, least of all a Scottish laird, went to Majorca in 1948. Perhaps it was fate. My father was very inclined to succumb to fate. In that, too, he was a typical lowland Scot. But he was canny in the other sense too. When I inherited the estate, I discovered I was wealthy – even if most of the funds were tied up in stocks and bonds and the like.

Ralph Peterswald, my father's solicitor, explained it all to me at length, but to be frank, I found it terribly boring and could tell you more about the view from his India Street third floor window in Edinburgh's professional quarter. I am like that. I have an eye for detail – the wrong detail, some would say. It is why I am drawn to writing, I suppose.

I took myself off on a world tour for a year, going to such out of the way places as Alaska and New Zealand. I meant to go to Morocco, but somehow never got there. Anyway, when I got home, Clare had married Stephen Wotherspoon, the local vicar. I couldn't imagine what had possessed her to do such a thing, but supposed she must have loved him. I was at a bit of a loose end after that. The house had taken on a sort of creepy emptiness. It was more than I could cope with.

The family estate is in that forever disputed land of the borders, near Eyemouth. To me, there was a complacent smugness about those fertile hills, as if they knew how much they were coveted by successive kings and queens from either side. We had a tenant farmer who was a sight more wedded to the land than I was. I suggested to Peterswald that we let the man run the whole show. He arched an arrogant brow at me and rather stupidly asked what my sisters thought of that. I told him it was none of their damned business – which was true. As an Edinburgh solicitor he, of all people, ought to have understood the power of a Scottish hereditary successor.

I took the matter into my own hands and struck a deal with the farmer, which was mutually beneficial. He was to move his family into the manor house to caretake it. He would also have the additional surrounding acres in return for a surcharge on the net profit. In a good season we would both benefit. We settled on a figure below which he would be freed of the surcharge. This was a necessary proviso to protect him from market downturns and poor seasons. I had no desire to bleed the poor fellow dry. After all, he was doing all the work.

He was now squire of the manor in all but name. We locked up a couple of the larger rooms so that I could store some of the more valuable pieces of family furniture and he had the run of the rest.

I took a flat in Edinburgh and began planning my life. I was 34 years old, single, footloose and fancy free as they say. I contemplated a course at university – language studies, perhaps. I had always been interested in the multiplicity of British dialects and their origins. In my own region the centuries-old love affair with the French language had thrown up some strange aberrations. Edinburgh's 'gardieloo' being an example. They had even named a street for it.

Connected to this interest was a growing desire to try my hand at writing. It was not as if I had a novel in my head or anything of that sort. It was more like a tick under my skin. An itch to make a start. I supposed the agenda would set itself once I put pen to paper, or a blank sheet of paper in my typewriter.

Having allowed this notion to take root, I soon came to realise my Edinburgh flat was a less than ideal place in which to focus the mind. For one thing, my friends kept turning up and dragging me off to the pub, or the theatre. Mornings were lost in coffee shops, or browsing the city's myriad bookshops. My time was never my own.

I am a keen fisherman – hence the attraction of Alaska and New Zealand. I began thinking of killing two birds with the one stone. I envisaged a remote cottage in a highland glen with a burn at the door and perhaps a loch nearby. Then I saw the advertisement for Westerfield in the *Scots Magazine*.

> 'Peaceful croft house in idyllic surroundings.
> Discover the magic of Shetland. Good fishing.
> Long lease desirable.'

I bought an ordnance survey map of the area. It showed every track and tarn, every croft house (even Westerfield), and all sorts of intriguing antiquities such as brochs, burnt mounds and cairns. I was hooked. I initially booked Westerfield for a month but extended it to six and later twelve. I seemed to have found my niche.

Although I set up my typewriter within minutes of entering the house, it was more a symbolic gesture than a serious statement of intent. There was a world of discovery waiting for me beyond the door. I sorted my groceries into the empty cupboards in the bottom of the dresser, smiling to myself as I discovered a jar of caviar on which Clare had stuck a hand-written label: 'For Emergency Use Only'. Now I knew what she had meant when she arrived at my flat with the hamper of goodies.

"There's a little something in there for when you tire of smoked mutton," she had said.

"Smoked mutton! God forbid!" I cried.

"Oh yes, my dear, Shetland is famous for it. It's called reestit mutton, and don't say I didn't warn you."

I didn't venture too far that first afternoon. The road continued past my cottage for about another half mile to a fork. The left turn was sign-posted 'Otter's Dale', while the right, which was little more than a footpath, was unsigned. I took the path that ended at a tumbling burn rushing out of the hills into a steep cleft. Following it down, I came on a tiny mill which had been ingeniously set to harness the maximum force of water. A short millrace diverted the flow to horizontal paddles which turned a shaft. The shaft extended upwards through a wooden floor where it was fixed to a small stone quern for grinding corn. Everything seemed to be in working order and as the roof was newly thatched, I assumed it was still used. I would have liked to see it in operation.

A profusion of wild flowers were strewn across the steep banks above the burn as though painted there in random splashes of colour. Besides primroses, which predominated, there were at least half a dozen other varieties. I found patches of squill set deep in the turf – sapphires on a cloak of velvet green. Higher up, looking like rouge on a dowager's cheek, blushes of thrift wafted their honeyed scent. Looking closer, I found the rarer Shetland orchids hiding in the long grass at the burn's edges – clusters of waxy flowers hanging down on thick stalks.

In the burn itself, where foam swirled into backwaters under the bank, I fancied trout were lurking. I would come this way again with my rod. For now, the fresh sea air was stirring up hunger pangs. It was time to head back. Out to sea a trawler was heading home with its attendant cloud of gulls. Judging by the frenzied activity in the wake, I concluded the crew must be gutting their catch.

Back at the croft house the Rayburn was fine and hot so I decided to make leek and potato soup. It would be worth waiting for. I busied myself peeling potatoes. Meanwhile, a good malt and a slice of rye with smoked salmon would keep me going. Clare's hamper was not going to last long.

I was clattering around the scullery checking out what utensils I had so I did not hear the knock on the door. The first I knew of my visitor was a mild voice at my elbow.

"Hello. I knocked but you were makin' such a din ... "

He pronounced 'knocked' in two syllables – knock-ed. It reminded me of a provincial English pronunciation I had heard, though the locality now eluded me. I was to discover many idiosyncrasies in the Shetland dialect. They still used 'du' for 'you', which was apparently from the Norn language spoken in the islands centuries before, while 'dee' seemed to derive from the old English 'thee'.

I straightened to find an elderly man dressed in what appeared to be his Sunday suit. For a moment I thought I was being visited by an over-zealous clergyman. He was lanky, with the weather-beaten looks of a man who had spent his life at sea, or perhaps trailing the hills after sheep. He had a friendly, open face and smiling blue eyes. He wore the suit as though it were a hair shirt, which caused me to amend my first impression.

"Peerie Jessie said you'd moved in Mr Graham, so I came by to invite you to the funeral tomorrow."

I wondered if I had heard right.

"I'm the kirk elder for this side o' the village. Lowrie Petersen." He extended a bony hand.

I looked for something to dry my hands on, wiped them on my jersey and shook his hand. "Glad to meet you," I said.

"It's auld Maisie Hirple, du keens (as if I ought to). Three o'clock at the kirk. Like I said, I do this side of the toun – with the invitations, like. Tommy Johnson does the ither side."

"I see ... " But of course I didn't. "However, I'm afraid I didn't know ... who did you say?"

"Maisie Hirple o' Punds ... that was. She was a puir done body. The wonder is she came through the winter. No-one thought she would. And here we are, with the best o' the simmer afore wis and she's no spared to see it." He shook his head as though despairing of the fickleness of God.

"Anyway, it's of no consequence you not knowin' her. You'll be very welcome I'm sure." Then with a tilt of the head and the sideways glance of a sheepdog casting wide for a ewe that may or may not belong to the flock, he added, "Graham is it? I don't suppose you're any kin to the Scalloway Grahams?"

"Not as far as I know," I said, trying not to smile.

I wondered just how far the word had spread in the three and a bit hours I had been resident in Bruntisdale.

That evening I pinned my ordnance survey map to the low-coomed ceiling above my bed and lay in the twilight familiarising myself with the locale. I found Punds and wondered if Maisie was lying in state in the parlour. (I learned later that it was the custom to place the coffin in the church overnight, as though the sanctity of the place might seep in in the nick of time and point the soul in the right direction.) I pinpointed the church up a side road.

Otter's Dale looked interesting, as did a ruined broch on the cliffs to the north. After that I wandered amongst the hill lochs (figurative speaking), intrigued by their names and wondering where the best fishing might be. I didn't like the sound of 'Sheep-dip Loch', but Nyuggel, Ramse, Shaela and Veskey Lochs deserved investigation, if only on account of their names.

The warmth from the Rayburn downstairs soon made me drowsy. I went to sleep with the sound of waves sighing back and forth on the steep pebble beach half a mile below the house.

I had not thought to bring a suit with me, but supposed a pair of grey flannels and a herringbone Aquascutum sports coat would have to do. As I knotted my least flamboyant tie – a burgundy silk Pierre Cardin – I practised mournful expressions in the mirror, wondering all the while at the wisdom of what I was doing.

I was never much of a one for funerals, being able to count the occasions on one hand. My father's, of course – on a day of teeming rain; an old school chum who had been killed mountaineering in Nepal, and a couple of uncles. And now Maisie Hirple, late of Punds. It was a bit of a joke really. And yet. This ought to be grist to a writer's mill. Besides, it wouldn't do to offend the sensibilities of Bruntisdale on day two. If it was the custom to invite strangers to their funerals, who was I to snub them. I wondered what other invitations might be in the offing.

The church was plain and unadorned. It would as readily have passed for a village hall or perhaps a school. The absence of the usual surrounding burial ground added to the secular appearance. I was to discover this was not uncommon.

Churches may come and go as people move their centre of activity from place to place, but burial grounds seem to be as eternal as the bones they keep. Bruntisdale graveyard was nearly two miles from the church on a lonely cliff top well away from all habitation. A tumble of stones in one corner hinted at an earlier building. Probably a priest's cell. It was the sort of place the first Christians seemed to favour.

I was told the coffin was carried from church to graveyard by successive foursomes in a long procession, but of course that was history. In recent times Young Bobby's van made the journey and only the immediate family and close friends witnessed the actual burial.

What awaited me inside the church was something of a culture shock. I had supposed three o'clock meant just that and arrived five minutes early to find the place packed and me the last man in. And I say 'last man' advisedly, for with the exception of the organist, the entire congregation was men. What is more, every single one was dressed from head to toe in black. There must have been close to a hundred there, all squeezed together, red-faced and sweating in the stuffy building.

The only available seat was at the front beside the organist. I very nearly turned tail and fled, but heads had turned and nodded soberly at me as though I was actually one of them. Nothing could be further from the truth. I stood out like a sore thumb in my frivolous grey. I felt judgmental eyes following me as I passed down the aisle through the assembly. My own eyes were firmly on the coffin lying below the altar. I might have been the prodigal, returned too late to find my mother died of a broken heart. It was ludicrous. Why was I feeling guilty? A sacrilegious interloper in this black sea of solidarity. If the floor had opened and swallowed me it would have been a welcome escape. I was glad to sink into my seat.

The organist slipped me a glance. I recognised Peerie Jessie from the shop, and would have smiled if she had, but she was too preoccupied with 'Amazing Grace'. The organ didn't appear to respond very well to pathos, being better suited, I imagined, to the 'Glory, Hallelujahs' of Sankey and Moody. It scarcely mattered, as no amount of sacred music, however well rendered, could penetrate the black silence that kept swallowing it up. I kept my head down.

The music stopped suddenly. Everyone stood up – a sort of collective sigh followed by awkward coughs. I looked up to see the minister had entered from a door behind the altar. Here, it appeared, was the ultimate irony. The parish minister was on holiday and the Church of Scotland had sent one of its new breed of locums, fresh out of Theological College. Yes, the all male congregation was about to be addressed by a woman!

Nor was this woman like one of their own. This was a jolly sort, dressed in bright red and decidedly larger than life. With the gay attire, came a sunny, cheerful disposition that would brook no gloom. Here was a species quite unknown in archconservative Bruntisdale where funerals were grave matters – if you'll pardon the pun.

To the Reverend Sheila Parry this was a new day. A day for joyous celebration. The coffin before her, far from being a symbol of grief, was a sure pointer to the eternal hope of the resurrection to come.

"Let us rejoice and sing," she said, in defiance of the threatening black cloud in front of her. But Maisie Hirple's last word on the matter had been to request the Twenty-third Psalm, and despite its words of confident hope and the Rev. Sheila's best attempt to proclaim them at a merry pace, with all the assurance she could muster, she was sorely outnumbered. Sing, they did. Rejoice, they did not.

The organist took her cue from the majority (as well she might), and the Psalm was sung as it had been sung in Bruntisdale for the past two hundred years (if not the past two thousand), with slow, measured dignity and exaggerated piety, as might be expected of crofters and seamen who knew better than to tempt providence when confronted with its awesome power; whether in tempest, fire, or still small voice.

I watched the minister closely, identifying with her battle of wits. It was plain she was no match for the united stubbornness before her. Yet I had to concede the right of these people to live their lives according to their own dictates. The church might wish to rule supreme in the lives of its people but it was increasingly being seen as dictatorial, if not downright irrelevant. The real irony in Bruntisdale, as far as I could judge, was not that the church had failed to move with the times, but that it had moved too far and too fast.

After the coffin had departed the crowd began to thin quickly. Here and there small knots of men stood chatting quietly. All were now wearing identical black caps. Mostly elderly and bent, they looked like so many crows descended on a harvest field in the hope of gleaning something. Feeling very much the subject of their covert glances, I made to slip away but Lowrie Petersen singled me out.

"So you came then." He seemed to be sizing me up.

"I gathered it was sort of expected."

"Na, na, Mr Graham, not at all. It's just the way we do things hereabouts. But you were wise to come for all that. It makes a difference to folks shows you understand."

"And if I hadn't come?"

"Och, you'd have been just as welcome in the village I dare say."

But I could tell from the way he said it that I had passed some sort of test.

"We'll maybe see you again on Sunday," he said with a wink.

"Eleven o'clock – though I'll take no responsibility for the sermon if you know what I mean. Our man's away for two weeks yet."

There was a wealth of feeling behind what was being said.

I told him I would bear it in mind and headed for my car. Peerie Jessie emerged from the vestry door as I was about to drive off. I hailed her.

"Can I give you a lift?"

"That'd be grand, thanks, if you care to, Mr Graham. Just to the turn-off will be fine. The minister picked me up," she said, settling herself into the seat. "But she'll be busy for a while at the putting down."

I didn't suppose she meant to be funny, but then again, perhaps she did. Shetlanders have a highly developed sense of humour.

"I presume there's a wake or some such," I said, wondering why I had not been invited to that also.

"Na, na," she remonstrated. "We don't go in for that sort of thing. We'll just keep the blinds down for a peerie start, till they've finished outby, then folks'll be out and about again I dare say."

I asked her about the 'men only' aspect.

"I don't rightly know," she said. "The lady minister was on about it too, saying it was a nonsense. But it's done us well enough for as long as anyone can remember. The womenfolk sit in – respectful lik, du keens, and if it's any way along the road to the graveyird, they keep their blinds doon in the front rooms. I suppose it dates from when they used to carry the remains all the way out. It was a man's job. Women would just be in the way."

There was a sort of logic in what she said but I couldn't help wondering how long it was since the practicality of the old way had ceased to have relevance. Perhaps it would take the permanent placement of someone like Sheila Parry to finally break down the taboos. She would have her work cut out if I was any judge.

"I take it you have another name besides Peerie Jessie," I ventured. I knew enough about village life to appreciate the importance of sorting out the who's who. Added to which, I could see Peerie Jessie's role, as postmistress and proprietor of the only shop, placed her in a unique position in the scheme of things.

"I've got several names, seein' you're asking."

I glanced at her quickly, as I thought by the sound of her voice I might have been taken for prying. But she was smiling.

"I started out Josephine Umphrey, only that wasn't yesterday. I was Joey for a while but that got changed to Jessie on account of my mam being Joey too. At school I got Peerie Jessie to differ me from Muckle Jessie who was in the same class. Young Bobby is my man, only he's actually Robert Smith. It was his aunt ... you know, the funeral. He's actually Robbie to me but everyone else calls him Young Bobby because Old Bobby – who's really Jimmy Peel – lives next door. You likely met him yesterday."

I nodded, thinking I was getting more than my money's worth for giving her the lift.

"Anyway, he gets Bobby on account of Peel – du keens. Though, if you ask me, it's daft."

Having got wound up, it appeared there was no stopping her.

"My Robbie has da contract for takin' the trawl catches from here o'er to da Scalloway fish factory. He goes twice a week. We've got five trawlers working out o' here, though da biggest een, *The Mareel*, generally goes tae Scalloway direct like, unless da weather is bad. Du keens it took us till half eleven da streen to clean da van oot. I telt Robbie aunty Maisie wouldn't mind da smell o' fish. She loved a nice piece o' North Bank's haddock when I had time to fillet it tae her. Here!" she cried, as I turned down towards the pier. "There's no need o' that. I can walk."

"It's no bother," I assured her. "Besides, I'm trying to work out what 'da streen' is."

Peerie Jessie clapped her hands to her face in embarrassment.

"Tch, dearie dear," she said shaking her head. "I niver was much at knapping. Da streen – that's last night, du keens. Some says yestreen."

"Of course! I should have picked up on that. It comes from Old English – yester evening – yestere'en. I am fascinated by language and the way it develops. I'm something of an etymologist I suppose."

Peerie Jessie looked at me as though I might be a bit daft in the head.

I pulled up outside the shop.

"But now you have given me another puzzle. What's knapping?" (She had pronounced both the 'k' and the 'n'.)

"Oh, that's what we call 'talking proper' – like we generally dae tae sooth-moothers – and before you ask, a sooth-moother is a visitor tae Shetland – someone who comes in on da *St Clair* tae Lerwick through da sooth mooth o' da harbour. Mind you, most comes by plane tae Sumburgh, so that's another daft sayin' o' wirs."

Peerie Jessie banged the car door shut then leaned back in through the open window. "We'll be open around sixish for a couple o' oors if you're needin' anything. Or du cud come alang in noo and tak a grain o' tae wi wis if du'd lik." The lapse into broad Shetland was probably meant as mischief but I told myself she was paying me a compliment.

I hesitated in replying – long enough for her to add, "Robbie'll be back fae da graveyird directly. I'm sure he'd like tae meet dee."

That clinched it. I thanked her and got out of the car.

When I look back on that first experience of Shetland hospitality, I realise the extent to which seemingly insignificant little things can make all the difference. My turning up at the funeral was undoubtedly a factor, then running Peerie Jessie to her door, rather than dropping her at the turn-off as she would happily have settled for, created the 'one good turn deserves another' response that is so much a part of their make up.

I was to discover Shetlanders never presume on your good nature. Their own natural reticence translates into an assumption that you will more than likely behave in a similar manner. If, however, you show the very least amount of consideration or do them any sort of little favour, they will immediately take you to their hearts and lavish all manner of kindness on you. It is as though their real selves are masked by a front of caution, a need borne of necessity to protect themselves from the unknown. This is not the dourness of the Scots – more a resignation to the way things are: a recognition that the land has formed them and, like it, their natures are subject to forces beyond their control. What visitors see as a drab sameness in the landscape, is in reality a perfect adaptation to the awesome forces of wind and weather. If the gales that sweep Shetland in winter were to visit the Florida Keys, for example, they would leave in their wake a trail of devastation. Trees would be uprooted, roofs blown off and fences flattened.

In Shetland the wind may howl in a chimney like a banshee, but it will seldom blow it down. It may tear the sea to shreds and dash it at the ragged cliffs, but it passes over the land with what seems to be a mutual understanding that neither will impede nor divert the other. The houses and animals are at one in their complicity with this. They have shaped themselves, or have been shaped, to the contours of the land. They make no demands, so none are made upon them.

All of nature has learned to live with the way things are. It knows when to break forth in joyous harmony with the sun, to celebrate life in all its complexities and colours. And it knows when to hold its peace and sink back into mother earth. So it seems to be with the people. They cloak themselves in a veneer of outward caution which may translate as shyness. They make no demands on what they readily accept as the natural order of things. There might even be an element in this of what they would call 'God's Will' – sometimes expressed in terms of 'It likely has to be'. But in their veins runs a stream of kindness and merriment which is ever ready to surface in their inherent generosity and which is readily translated into their love of fast and furious music. Shetlanders never take themselves too seriously. They love to 'tak a fun', whether at their own expense or another's.

Because Peerie Jessie had already taken me in, as it were, Young Bobby was the soul of geniality from his first handshake.

"You'll tak a dram," he said before he had removed his coat. And so began a most pleasant evening. Young Bobby was fair and handsome with those clean-cut features that marked him as being of Viking stock. The dram of whisky he handed me was a generous three-finger measure. It seemed to be indicative of his nature. There was a merry twinkle in his blue eyes with mischievous lines at their corners. You would hardly have imagined he was newly returned from burying his aunt.

We had a light meal at five-thirty then Jessie opened the shop at six. She was back at seven, saying the weather had taken a turn for the worse and there would likely be no more folk venturing forth. I was introduced to 'eight-o'clocks' – a sort of mid-evening repast that was not to be confused with supper, which in all probability would materialise a couple of hours later. I soon discovered one needed a powerful constitution to withstand the onslaught of tea, bannocks, biscuits and cake that seemed to flow hourly in Shetland hospitality.

Eight-o'clocks generally consisted of a plate with a variety of goodies on it – thick ham sandwich, buttered water biscuit, scone or pancake, a slab of cake and couple of iced fancies. You were expected to eat the lot. Failure to do so invoked genuine concern. "What ails dee, lad? Du hes tae keep dee strent up." Though for what, was a mystery. It was past midnight when I made it back to my croft house. It was to be the first of many such memorable evenings – some lasting into the wee small hours, for Shetlanders are never in a hurry to seek their beds.

The weather had deteriorated further by morning. I lay in bed listening to the rain lashing on the skylight and was grateful for the comforting warmth from the Rayburn downstairs.

The Smiths had had a peat fire in a big open grate complete with inglenook. When the temperature fell late in the evening, Young Bobby had upended half a barrow load of peats into the hearth then stacked them expertly in a cone shape, which was soon blazing to create a whistling draught round my ankles while making my cheeks glow. He told me a weird tale of shipwreck, prompted by Peerie Jessie emptying the dregs of the teapot onto the fire. It was an old tale which I imagine had been much embroidered with the telling.

A ship, bound out of Dublin for Murmansk in Russia, with jute and linen, had been driven off course in a gale. Attempting to clear the island known as the Noss of Bruntisdale, it had broken a rudder chain and lost steerage. Within minutes the vessel was in mortal danger. The crew had tried to run her between two large rocks in the hope of climbing to safety. There was no hope of lowering boats in the maelstrom.

At the last moment the ship had swung broadside and been flung viciously on her beam. The rigging had come crashing down, sweeping many men into the sea where their end was mercifully swift. Others were trapped below the hatches and drowned as the ship began breaking up under the relentlessly pounding waves.

A young lad, waiting his chance to get clear, had been clinging to the bowsprit when it snapped like a carrot and carried away cleanly. The boy, calling the Blessed Virgin's name over and over, clung for dear life as the sea engulfed him.

In the lee of the ship the spar surfaced with its half-drowned cargo, but the boy barely had time to take breath before a huge wave swept in between the ship's hull and the cliff face. Like a giant switchback, the sea was forced up and up, before breaking through the gap and flinging the bowsprit forward like a spear.

The impetus carried the spar high onto the beach where it crashed amongst the rocks jarring every tooth in the lad's head and breaking both his wrists. He fell with a moan and was almost dragged back by the surge. Somehow he kept his footing amongst the slippery rocks and managed to stagger to beyond the high-water mark where he fell gasping on a mountain of kelp.

The young seaman must have lost consciousness then, for the first he remembered was waking in the pitch dark (the ship had been wrecked in the late afternoon), and hearing nothing but the crash of waves and the moaning of the wind. His wrists were swollen and burning with pain. All else was besieged by cold such as he had never endured. His tongue was swollen so that he could scarcely close his mouth and he had a raging thirst. Despite the excruciating pain it caused him, the boy tried to burrow into the kelp and to some degree was successful. It was to be his salvation.

In the early morning, Davie Thomason, who lived in an isolated house near the cliff top, was preparing to set out in search of a pony that had strayed. As he was pulling on his boots by the fire, his wife took a scoomer (a flat spoon) and skimmed some froth from the top of a soup-kettle hanging on a swee over the flame.

The woman tipped the scoomer's contents onto the fire, dousing a peat standing out from the others. Davie, seeing what she had done, admonished her. "Hey, lass! Du's near as droonded the stranger who's come seeking oor hearth."

His wife laughed, but she pushed the peat nearer the fire to dry it. She did not want to be responsible for a catastrophe.

Davie set out for the hill with his collie at his heels. The wind had dropped overnight and a sea fog had swirled in to reduce visibility to a few yards. It was folly to go, yet he continued, drawn towards the cliffs with a sense of impending doom hanging over him as thickly as the mist.

The dog saw something first – or sensed it, and started to growl. Davie stopped, peering ahead into the mist. A figure materialised before him, coming from where no human being could. Beyond him were the cliffs and the Atlantic Ocean far below. Davie called out in fear and dread, "Are you earthly or unearthly?" for he was certain he was seeing a ghost. The boy – for it was he – was at the point of collapse and could scarcely articulate anything coherent. He seemed to say "earthly," then contradict himself by sobbing, "the sea – the sea has taken them all." He fell in a swoon at Davie's feet.

The collie nuzzled the boy gently then looked anxiously at its master. The action seemed to reassure Davie for he lifted the slight figure and carried him home. It remained a mystery how the boy had climbed the cliff. It had never been done before. When it became known both his wrists were broken, people said it was a miracle.

I was to hear the same story from others in different parts of Shetland. Sometimes the wreck was on Sumburgh Head, most frequently on the island of Foula. The details varied, but always the folklore of the peat fire was an essential element. I came to wonder if Peerie Jessie had deliberately thrown the tea-leaves in the fire to invoke the tale.

Chapter Two

I breakfasted late, savouring the palate-cleansing tang of Keilor's thick cut marmalade which stimulated a mind picture of orange groves along the upper Murray River in Australia. I could smell the fruit on the trees. It had been a spur of the moment detour out of Melbourne on my way to New Zealand. My companion on the plane was from the orange growing district of Renmark, near Mildura and his description of the place, coupled with a generous invitation to stay a couple of nights on his farm, was too good to refuse.

The Murray River begins its journey in the Southern Alps of New South Wales and travels inland for several hundred miles, forming the border between Victoria and New South Wales. About sixty miles beyond Mildura, on the border with South Australia, the river takes a sharp bend southward, eventually emptying into the Indian Ocean below Adelaide in what is known as the Great Australian Bight. Renmark is situated on the river bend. It is a hot, dry region of Australia, ideal for growing oranges. The groves spreading out on either side of the broad river almost as far as the eye can see.

I was greatly taken with the region, promising myself I would return one day to hire a houseboat and cruise along the Murray. It looked like it might be a lot of fun and the size of the Murray cod had to be seen to be believed. All the houses had wide verandas to shade their windows from the glare of the sun. Every surface was a reflector – the red clay soil; the unpainted corrugated iron roofs; the cars (which all appeared to be white Fords or Holdens), and of course the glossy expanse of the river. Even the shiny leaves on the trees reflected bright light, and as the temperature rose, the air became filled with the essence of oranges.

The extent to which a spoonful of flavour can evoke such intense sensual responses never ceases to amaze me. The stronger or rarer the flavour, the more powerful the image. Marmalade on a jaded palate never fails to do the trick. The memory jolt was in sharp contrast to the view from my croft house window. I say view, but in reality there was no view. The rain clouds had descended to obliterate all but the road, which now looked more like a shiny black river. It was definitely not a day for venturing forth.

It seemed as though the gods were telling me I had run out of excuses for postponing my chief purpose in being here. The typewriter was in front of me, a ream of paper beside it. I had Biros and notebooks with which to jot down random thoughts. I had my *Shorter Oxford*. My *Roget's Thesaurus*. It was crunch time. I made some fresh coffee and took up station at my 'desk', flexing my fingers as though I might be about to undertake a delicate operation.

I put a blank sheet of paper in the typewriter and stared at it ...

Half an hour later I was still staring and the coffee was stone cold. This would not do at all.

The problem was I had no clear idea of what I wanted to write about. Ever since my school days I had messed about at writing short stories. I had even succeeded in having a couple published in magazines. But always, in the back of my mind, was the urge to do something more substantial. No doubt it was presumptuous of me, but I really believed I had at least one novel in me. It was why I had travelled – broadening the mind, as they say.

I had chosen Alaska in particular because it represented the edge of civilisation to me. No doubt the Alaskans would not be flattered by my assessment of their state, but what I really mean is they seem to have retained some of their frontier mentality. A last tinge of gold fever in their veins, perhaps. I had read James Michener's epic tale and been inspired to discover more. I was not disappointed. The towering majesty of the mountains. The pristine forest and mighty rivers. Everything needed a superlative – or several of them – to be adequately described. Even the mosquitoes were bigger and more vicious than anywhere else. The souvenir shops sold novelty mosquito traps and the locals told jokes about unwary tourists being carried off bodily. There was the stuff of a whole library of books to be gleaned, if one was only skilled enough to write them.

In New Zealand also, especially the South Island, I found pockets of that same edge of excitement. Even though the people were third and fourth generation New Zealanders, they still had an adventurous, almost pioneering spirit. They had a sort of raw courage too. I think they call it the 'Anzac Spirit'. I thought it probable this 'never say die' attitude was what made their national rugby team so formidable.

In the back of my mind was the germ of an idea which I hoped would grow into something workable. It was based around a stint I had had on a sheep station near Arrowtown, in southern New Zealand. I had happened on the place at shearing time and they were short-handed. What started as a week's frenzied work, gathering up the fleeces and sweeping the board in the shearing shed, had ended up becoming three months as a general farmhand. I spent the greater part of that time bouncing around on a tractor as we tried to get the winter oats sown before the rains came. On weekends I had explored the surrounding region, venturing into Skippers Gully. It was the one place Avis had said I must not take their hire car. At least, if I did, it would not be covered by insurance.

Skippers was the sort of 'edge of excitement' place I was looking for. A steep ravine with a treacherous road cut into the face of the cliff. In several places wash-aways had rendered it virtually impassable. I should explain. I did it on horseback. To attempt it with the car would have been suicidal. A yellow river snaked its way through the canyon. It was a long way down. In places tall trees reached up from the narrow riverbank, but mostly it was bare rock and ochre clay, slashed bright under the shafted sun. Eventually the road reached the bottom.

Although Skippers had been the centre of a gold rush a century earlier, there was little evidence of it now. Most of the diggings had been washed away in the flash floods that were a feature of the place. The bridge that had once spanned the narrows was gone too, leaving only rusty supports in the cliffs on either side and a jagged tooth of timber in the middle of the stream.

There were the remains of a collapsed derrick partially blocking a dangerous looking hole in the ground. Nearby the usual 'Dangerous – Keep Out' sign. There had been some tunnelling in the cliff face – all boarded up now and similarly signed. A few concrete foundations with rusty bolts sticking out of them. A last sheet of tin flapping on the skeletal remains of a hut, clacking and rasping in alien accompaniment to the quiet murmur of the stream. I had been told it was a lively place in its heyday though the gold had panned out quickly.

As in all such places, there remained an air of expectancy, as if the cliffs and river had conspired to keep the best to themselves. You instinctively knew there just had to be some gold there still. It made the hairs stand up on the back of your neck and your blood tingle. There were pages of my unwritten book to be dredged out of that gully. Gold, of a sort.

More pages fluttered up and down the streets of Arrowtown with its restored blacksmith's shop, its picturesque tree-lined streets and quaint cottages. The boarded up old hotels with their deep-shaded balconies, all elaborately decorated with wrought-iron lacework, positively oozed intrigue and romance. It needed little imagination to conjure up a tale. And then there was the sheep station. Surely it would provide the characters and perhaps the plot. All that was needed was a catalyst. Something to set in motion the thought processes. It would come. I never doubted it.

Peerie Jessie's word for talking with in-comers came to mind. 'Knapping'. I thought it extremely unlikely that my *Oxford Dictionary* would have anything on it. I was wrong. I found a number of meanings for 'knap', including the one I was looking for. It was defined as 'to speak clearly'. However the examples given implied correct enunciation of English as opposed to provincial dialects. James of Scotland, when hearing some one 'knapping suddrone', was said to have condemned him for a traitor.

When I had discussed the word further with Young Bobby, it was plain that the Shetland understanding of it had a similar element of treachery attached. While it may be polite to knap in certain circumstances, to do so unnecessarily was, at the very least, to give oneself airs and at worst to be currying favour.

I took up one of my notebooks and began what was to become quite an extensive list of words that were new to me. The first word was 'peerie', which, though not strictly speaking new to me, seemed to have additional meanings in Shetland. My maternal grandmother was from Fife and as a child I had often heard her use the word. I supposed it came from the French petite which had much the same meaning. (The word has fallen from usage on the Scottish mainland where it appears to have been confined mainly to the east coast.)

Besides the common meaning of 'small', the Shetlanders used the word as a verb. "Gang du peerie-wyes," a woman told her youngster who was thumping up the stairs to bed. The child immediately quietened his step. I liked the sense of gentleness that was implied in the expression.

The rain eased to a drizzle in the afternoon, by which time the kitchen had become hot and stuffy. I decided to don wet weather gear and go out for a newspaper. I had a miscellany of random jottings in my notebook along with a memory sketch of an otter. It was better than nothing, even if the sheet of paper in the typewriter continued to present me with a disconcertingly blank stare.

By the time I reached the pierhouse the drizzle had ceased and the sun was making a valiant attempt to shoulder its way out of the clouds. Old Bobby was out on his bench, though I supposed he could not have been there long. Perhaps he saw himself as a real life version of one of those Dutch weather indicators where a man and his wife stand at two doors of a dinky model cottage. The wife popping out in a sunbonnet on fine days and the man in a sou'wester on rainy days. I looked in vain for Old Bobby's partner.

He gave me a barely perceptible nod as I passed. I noticed he was carving something intricate in his lap. It looked as though it might be a piece of driftwood, smoothed and bleached by the sea. I would have stopped to look, but there was something intimidating about the man. Though I glanced into his face, I was still unable to make out the colour of his eyes.

Peerie Jessie told me I was an hour too early for the papers. Apparently Young Bobby generally arrived with them at 5pm. She offered me the previous day's *Scotsman*, which I declined. To fill in the time I decided to extend my walk and return later.

I strolled down the pier. It was a broad concrete breakwater, wide enough to drive a truck along, extending some hundred and fifty yards out into the bay. A trawler was unloading boxes of fish about halfway along. They were being stacked on a handcart. I stopped to watch, feeling like a tourist, which I suppose I was in a way. A fisherman in oilskins dumped a box and came over to me. He had a knitted woollen cap on his head and a bushy ginger beard.

"You the cove that's taken Westerfield?" he asked.

"Yes, that's me. Stuart Graham." It no longer surprised me that everyone seemed to know all about me.

He removed a grubby glove and offered his hand.

"Tom Renwick," he said, giving my hand a strong grasp. "I knew all about you before you crossed the grid. Westerfield's my grandmother's place. I hope you like it."

I assured him I liked it very much.

"Any problems, you see my Greta. The last house at the end of the loch there." He pointed out a rooftop about a mile away to the south. "It's called North Hoose. Yes, I know," he added, seeing the involuntary arch of my brow. "Some of the old folks got a bit confused about their compass. Still, I suppose it's north of somewhere. Depends on your point of view, doesn't it? Anyway, the old man I bought it from wouldn't know his arse from his elbow. Fancy a couple of haddock for your tea?"

"I certainly would," I said.

"These are North Bank haddock." He had crossed over to the stacked boxes where he selected two plump fish, holding them up for approval. "Peerie Jessie says they're the best and she should know, she's filleted more than I've caught in a lifetime at sea. She used to follow the fleet in the days when herring were all the go. Started at Hull and Lowestoft and worked her way north."

He pulled a plastic carrier bag from a container tied to the side of the trolley and slid the fish in. "Tell you what," he added, grabbing three more fish. "Take the lot down to her with my compliments and tell her I said to do a couple for you."

I pulled my wallet from my back pocket but he brushed it aside with a wave of his hand.

"Na, na. There's no need for that. We'll just let the Scalloway fish factory take care of that side of things. There's always a fish for you at the end of the pier – with or without a line." He winked, then glanced up towards the pierhouse. "I see Ould Bobby's got the glasses on us. Nosy ould bugger. He'll be along directly, like a greedy maa, wantin' his share."

I thanked him profusely and headed back up the pier.

“Mind and give Greta a call if you need anything,” he shouted after me.

I left the fish with Peerie Jessie then headed south along the high-water mark. The loch looked small but there might be fish in it. I should have asked Tom. The beach was littered with pieces of tarry wood and knotted ends of frayed and bleached orange nylon rope. There were pieces of broken glass bottles, milky green and brown, ground down by sea and sand into collectible objet d’art. I pocketed a couple for my desk.

On the tide-line, in drifts of seaweed, were the usual ubiquitous plastic bottles and the odd sandshoe. There were pink and orange sea-urchin shells too, some quite large and unbroken. As the upper end of the beach was rough and stony, it was a marvel so many had survived intact. Oyster-catchers were running ahead of me piping their metallic alarm calls, like the clink of a hammer on an anvil. There were Arctic terns also, diving angrily at my head. Their nests would be around my feet. I would need to tread with care. I moved further back from the beach to give the birds a little more space, but they continued to dive-bomb me, screeching their indignation.

A number of piles of driftwood had been carefully stacked. Planks and fish boxes, with the occasional green glass buoys in their rope meshes. I was aware of the beachcomber’s law which held that all jetsam was designated ‘finders keepers’. Once gathered and placed above the high-water mark, however, it was deemed to be the private property of the salvager.

In one place a rutted track had been cut through to the shore, the chunky treads of a tractor tyre indicating someone had been recently gathering seaweed to spread on their rigs. It made a rich fertilising mulch which did wonders for the soil. My father used to buy drayfuls of the stuff from an enterprising fellow in Eyemouth, until the practise was outlawed because of the damage being done to the foreshore.

By this time, the clouds were breaking up and moving away beyond the hills to the south-east. Westward was clearing sky and the promise of a fine night. The sea had been flattened by the rain. Inshore it was grey/green, moving desultorily in a long, low swell. Further out patches of aqua-tone marked the sunlight, while cloud-shadow showed up as deep navy blue.

A couple of seals were watching my progress from the safety of deep water. Probably waiting to come ashore for a roll in the sand. They looked like inquisitive Labradors, thrusting their noses skywards to catch my alien scent. Beyond them, a mile or so offshore, I could just make out two or three small islands, low-lying and indistinct against the sheen of the sea.

The loch was close to the sea behind a dune which had been sliced through by a narrow burn. The peat-brown water ran sluggishly out of the cutting and across a pebbled beach. From loch to sea, the burn was no more than fifty yards long with grassy overhanging banks. Sea trout would run up here in the autumn. More than likely the locals netted it, even though it was illegal. The loch itself looked shallow as far as I could tell, with a small island in the centre. I would need my waders if I were to attempt any fishing as the entire circumference was choked with reeds, bog bean and flag irises. It did not look promising. I knew there would be another burn entering at the top so began walking round to check it out.

A tractor was moving slowly along a ploughed rig on the slope to my right. Someone was sitting on a platform behind. Planting potatoes, I guessed. A waft of diesel fumes reached me. An alien smell amongst the sea-wrack. The driver waved as he turned at the bottom of the furrow. I waved back. It gave me a nice feeling. As though I belonged. In my part of Scotland, and even more so over the border, I would have been taken for a trespasser. More than likely the wave would have been a shaken fist or at the very least an angry enquiry as to 'what the hell I was doing there'.

There were two houses side by side at the head of the loch. I couldn't be sure which was Tom's as the road, where presumably the name would be on a gate, was behind them. I kept to the lochside until I had passed the second house. This was where the burn I was looking for ran in. It was deep and dark, with cut away sides rather as if it might be man-made – probably to drain the low-lying field further east. A sturdy timber bridge with a handrail on one side gave access to a path on the opposite bank. The path led towards high cliffs which formed the boundary of the toun on this side. I would save that walk for another day.

I took the path back on my side and found it led to the road-end. The first house was a modern bungalow. It had its name, 'The Loch', in a semicircle of gold letters across the fanlight above the door. A bit of logic for once, or a case of stating the obvious. The next house must be North Hoose.

A woman was feeding a flock of large speckled hens in the roadway. I paused to say, "Good evening." Perhaps I could turn the table for a change and say, "You must be Greta," but I thought she might take offence at being addressed thus by a stranger. I admired her hens instead.

"They're Plymouth Rocks," she said. "They lay bonnie speckled eggs. I could sell you some if you'd like."

"I'd like that fine."

Here was a chance for a formal introduction. She picked up her pail and headed back towards 'The Loch'.

"I'm Elsie," she called over her shoulder. "You'll be Mr Graham."

Foiled again.

There was no sign of life at North Hoose when I set off home with my purchase. Greta was probably the one sowing potatoes off the back of the tractor down by the loch. In the manner of Shetland life, the hour of day or night had nothing to do with the task being undertaken. As like as not, Greta would not get her supper till the job was done. Perhaps 10pm if I was any judge of the remaining rig to be ploughed.

Back at the shop, I picked up my newspaper and fish fillets, thanking Peerie Jessie for her kindness. She handed me a packet of Ruskoline. "Toss the fillets in some of that and fry them. You'll not taste finer this side of heaven."

She was right.

Chapter Three

Apart from one sunny day, which I spent stumbling through heather from loch to loch in a reconnoitring foray to establish likely fishing spots, the rest of that week was wet and windy. I stayed close to home, doing a good deal of pencil chewing and random jotting in notebooks. I also typed a few pages of disconnected narrative which made me feel less of a fraud.

On the Saturday night I telephoned Clare from the call-box at the pierhead (there was no phone in the cottage). I told her I was going to stay for at least another six months.

"Are you sure?" she said. "You've only been there a week."

I could picture her furrowed brow. Ever since our mother departed the scene, Clare had taken on the role of surrogate mother.

"Absolutely sure. If I am ever going to write something, this is where it will happen. The cottage is perfect, the natives are friendly but don't impose, and it rains so much I am forced to stay indoors and get on with it."

"Oh well, in that case I had better send you another hamper!"

Did I say Clare mothered me? Actually that is not, strictly speaking, correct. Let's face it, she is only three years my senior. When mother left us in Majorca, you might imagine it was a terrible shock. Not really. We were well used to fending for ourselves. Mother had no maternal instincts. If she had been a bird I fancy she would have shoved us out of the nest and set about preening herself.

My sisters and I were bottle-fed by a nanny. If we were lucky, mother came and tucked us in at night before turning off the light. Come to think of it, her turning off the light more or less sums up my mother's role in my life. In the ensuing years of darkness I have forgotten what she looked like.

Clare reckons it was three days before we twigged to the fact Mother had actually left us, but that is not true. I distinctly remember standing on a threadbare carpet in the lounge of our dingy hotel (incidentally, they had no idea how to cook porridge), and mother saying, "I'm going away, children." She tended to address us collectively. It saved repetition and avoided alarming eye contact. Like politicians at press conferences, it also makes it easier to side-step the awkward questions. I think they call it 'fielding'. (If they drop the catch they simply claim the sun was in their eyes.)

I asked an awkward question. I asked, "Why?"

Mother chose to ignore me and instead directed a remark to Clare about her being the oldest and therefore responsible. Yes, that is what she said. "You're responsible now, Clare."

Then she kissed us. At least she kissed me. I can't be sure about my sisters. I recall there was a surfeit of lipstick because, when mother had gone, Clare spat on her hankie and rubbed my cheek. She mopped up my tears too, by which it was clear I understood what was happening to us. After that, father materialised from somewhere and took us all for a swim followed by ice cream.

What I meant by Clare's mothering, was essentially a mutual recognition of our need to look out for one another. Back at Eyemouth she took to coming and sleeping with me for a while, though whether for my comfort or her own, I am uncertain. Shortly afterwards, father bought us ponies and we transferred much of our yearning for affection to them. I could pour out my heart to my pony in the certainty that the tears he shed were tears of understanding.

Later in life, when the subject of my mother came up in conversation with outsiders, I generally said she had died when I was a child. In a sense it was true enough. Sometimes though, with friends at university for instance, I'd say, "Oh, she ran off with a Bavarian duke when I was three!" I enjoyed the response, especially from the girls, who immediately imagined themselves picking up the forlorn toddler and cuddling him. "You poor wee thing," they'd say, once they had made sure I wasn't pulling their leg.

I turned the villain into a Bavarian duke because I had come to realise Hungarian counts were a dime a dozen. Reducing my age to three seemed, to me, to make my mother's callousness all the more reprehensible and assure me of maximum sympathy. It got me off to an excellent start with quite a few girls.

It is true I have forgotten what my mother looked like. The face that tucked me in at night always had the light behind it, blurring the features. I have created a mind picture for myself. A sort of identikit image which has evolved over the years to become glamorised into someone akin to Grace Kelly. Clare reckons mother looked more like Maggie Thatcher, but that can't be right. Can you imagine a Hungarian count falling for Maggie Thatcher? In the absence of further evidence I am sticking to my image.

Where was I ... ?

Oh yes, fielding Clare's offer of additional sustenance. "No need," I said. "The fish just jump out of the sea into my frying-pan and judging by the planting that's going on around here, there will be tatties and neeps going begging by the ton, to say nothing of the famous reestit mutton, which I have yet to sample."

"Very well, but you'll let me know if you need any oranges won't you. I'd hate you to go down with scurvy."

"Very droll, Clare. I'll have you know, my kaleyard is shoulder high with nettles, rhubarb and dockens. I'm making a witches brew to cure all ills."

"Super! Send me a bottle," she said. "It might fix my poor Stephen's haemorrhoids."

She was always making outrageous remarks like that – usually at the dinner table when they were entertaining the bishop, or some snobbish woman Clare thought needed taking down a peg or two.

When Clare was a little girl of four, mother had been persuaded to hostess an afternoon tea party at the manor in order that the new parish rector might meet some of the gentry. The rather nervous priest had dropped a buttered scone in his lap. Clare, assuming he would deliver himself of an expletive, as father most certainly would have done, wagged a finger in the unfortunate fellow's face.

"Don't say damn and blast," she admonished. "Don't say hell's teeth. Don't say bugger it. Don't say sh ... "

At this point (so the story goes), mother had the presence of mind to ram a cream cake in Clare's mouth and send her out to play. Legend has it that Clare's extensive vocabulary of swear words could make the proverbial sailor blush. Perhaps she had married Stephen to make certain he kept to the straight and narrow. No wonder he had haemorrhoids.

On the Sunday afternoon I drove out to North Hoose where I found Tom Renwick painting his porch door. (It seems the days of Sabbath rest had fled even this remote corner of Christendom.)

Tom greeted me warmly and invited me in but I declined. I knew the frustration of an interrupted painting job. As a fisherman he would have little enough time for catching up on jobs around the house.

"I just wanted to arrange an extension on my lease," I said. "If it's okay with your grandmother, I'd like to stay until the end of December."

"I imagine she'd be delighted. I'll give her a call and let you know." He put his brush down and stood back to admire his handiwork. "What do you think?"

A purple door with yellow trim wasn't my idea of taste, but the gaudier the better seemed to be the rule in these parts. I lied and told him it looked great.

He grinned, then, reading my mind he said. "Na. It's no my cup o' tae either, but what Greta wants, Greta gets."

As he took up his brush once more, I made to go, but he stopped me.

"You might want to think of getting some more peats if you're stayin' on intae the winter. What's in the byre won't last you long."

I explained that I was making do with the oil-fired Rayburn and didn't think I'd use the other room much. He agreed my decision, saying half the village had done away with peats, including himself. "Though I must admit," he added, "the electric's no match for a guid lowin' fire of a winter's night. We're a lazy lot of buggers when it comes down to it."

I thought he was selling himself short.

I did not take my fishing rod when I went to explore the lochs. I wanted to cover as much ground as possible so settled for a knapsack with a cheese sandwich and my Baby Leica camera.

I drove a couple of miles beyond the grid, to where the road levelled out on a small plateau. A red mini van was parked in a sort of quarry in front of a pile of pink granite gravel. There was a stack of tar barrels beside a tiny wooden shed. As I pulled up, a man came from behind the shed buttoning his trouser fly. I took him for a roadman.

"Fine day," I ventured.

"Fine day for casting peats, if that's what you mean," he said. He picked up a rather odd looking tool from beside his car. It had a straight wooden handle with a sharp blade protruding at right-angles from one end.

"Is that what you use to cut peat?" I asked.

"Yus," he said and spat on his hands, before taking a fresh grip, as though he might be contemplating disembowelling me with the thing. "It's called a tushkar. I'm joost away tae da hill tae cast up a few."

He was a funny looking fellow. A bit bandy-legged and stooped. A shock of white hair thrusting out on all sides of a leathery face that had more wrinkles than a prune. He had beady black eyes and a hook of a nose. His teeth were badly stained – the ones he had, for at least half were missing. He was quite short and I fancied he might pass for one of the legendary trows who were said to reside in these hills. The Shetland cousins of the Norwegian trolls. Perhaps he *was* a trow and I was about to be spirited away to never be heard of again. But I did not think trows drove red mini vans.

"Mind if I come and take a look?" I asked.

"Whit's tae mind? Suit yersel'."

I thought introductions might be in order. "I'm Stuart Graham," I offered.

"Yus, I keen." He spat on his hands again then set off across the moor. If he had a name he was in no hurry to divulge it. I grabbed my camera and took off after him.

We stopped at a sort of ditch where some peats had already been cut. The procedure, as I watched, was not unlike quarrying, only the working face was more vegetable than mineral. To begin with a top layer of turf was removed horizontally in big slabs about two feet square. This is done with a spade. These are carefully placed in the lower level where the previous year's peats have been cut. The turf takes root and continues to grow.

The depth of the quarry face varied, I was told, depending on the quality of the peat. However, there is a limit as to how far one can dig down into the bowels of the earth and still lift the saturated peat out. Six feet seems to be about the maximum depth. As each peat is cut out vertically to a depth of about fifteen inches, this means about four cuts plus the top turf.

The first two or three levels are thrown or 'cast' onto the top bank, while the last layer goes the opposite way onto the repositioned turf. I noticed the first level of peat tended to be brown in colour with a good proportion of root material. Apparently it is inclined to crumble when dry.

Progressive layers became darker and denser having been compacted by the weight of moor above them. These, I learned, dry to an almost coal-like consistency. Peerie Jessie had called these 'blue' peats, telling me they were the best. They burn very hotly and leave a white powdery ash like talcum.

As the peat hill contains a great amount of water, the work is heavy and time consuming. The peats have to be dried progressively; first in a dyke or wall, so structured as to leave gaps for the ever-present wind to blow through; then in loosely constructed stookies that might require turning several times depending on the weather. Sometimes, in a wet summer, the peats do not dry at all.

I watched the strange little man for a while as he established a sort of rhythm, slicing through the bank and swinging the tushkar in a fluid arc to land the soggy peats in a neatly spaced layer at my feet. The longer I watched, the more trow-like he became, until he seemed to be a part of the very hill itself.

That day I went as far north as Tors Lake which, though quite large, was overgrown with weeds. The only loch beyond this was Bratwater, but I had already decided I would visit it by walking up Brat Burn from the mill I had found on my first day. According to my map, there was a ruined broch on the cliffs beyond Bratwater. It should make for an interesting outing.

Returning southwards, my progress was considerably impeded by deep heather which concealed water-filled ruts and hollows. I was soon soaked to the knees. I fell flat on my face several times, startling a skylark off its nest on one occasion. The nest was made of long strands of dry grass and was about the size and shape of a tennis ball, with a very small opening slightly to one side. I peeped in. There were four exquisite little eggs looking like miniatures of the blue dome above me.

Eventually I reached a ridge of clearer ground. Climbing to a small cairn I could see a wide panorama before me. Directly below, sparkling in the sunlight was Nyuggel Loch, while further out to my left was Ramse Loch. Beyond them I could just make out the line of the road.

When I had set out from the quarry I passed through a gully between the two lochs and had not seen them at all. It occurred to me how easily one could become lost in these hills, particularly if the weather turned foul, as it frequently did. A person could blunder about for days, or more probably stumble into one of those treacherous holes under the heather and break a leg. It might be long enough before anyone found you. I hoped my little peat-cutting trow had taken note of which way I had gone. Not that I was really perturbed. It was a perfect day. I had my map with me and for the time being knew exactly where I was.

Nyuggel Loch looked promising. It was deep and dark with high banks to cast a line from. There were no streams running in or out of it, which raised the question of how trout would come to be there in the first place. I knew from experience, however, that such lochs did have trout, though how remained a mystery to me. I also knew that because of their landlocked nature, these lochs frequently had some unusually large fish in them. I gave Nyuggel a definite thumbs up. Later, when I found out the name meant a mythical waterhorse, I became even more interested in the loch.

In time I caught some very nice trout there, but nothing of any significant size. Eventually I concluded the nearness to the road was a mixed blessing. If I could get there easily, so could others. The big fish had probably all been caught.

Back at the quarry there was no sign of my trow or his van. So much for keeping a lookout for me. It was only a little after midday so I set out to explore the lochs south of the road. I passed several unnamed ones – all small and not likely to be worth fishing.

Shaela Loch was larger, with a couple of islands. It was in a lovely setting, a steep hill on the southern side casting a dark shadow across the water. The edges were mossy and the water was clear of weeds. A stream running in at the eastern end had some deep, black pools. All my fishing instincts were aroused by what I observed.

I was surprised to see a lone whooper swan glide out from the lee of the first island. I knew these birds migrated from beyond the Arctic Circle to winter throughout Britain, but they return to their breeding grounds in spring. This one must either have been injured, or perhaps its mate had died and it had remained beside the dead bird until the urge to depart had ceased.

Whooper swans mate for life and seem to grieve the loss of a partner much as humans do. The lone swan gave a tragic fairy-tale quality to Shaela Loch for me. (It was still there when I returned with my rod a few weeks later.)

I skirted the hill and continued south to check out Veskey Loch which was the largest on my map. It was another beautiful stretch of water curving under Skrotti Hill. It was here I came upon my first red-throated diver's nest. A bird-watcher's guide I had picked up on the Aberdeen-Lerwick ferry had mentioned these birds were quite rare in Britain. Photographing their nest was illegal. Nevertheless, as I had found the nest purely by chance and the bird seemed disinclined to leave it, I took a hurried snapshot before backing off and leaving the bird in peace. Who was to know, I thought.

To tell the truth, it did not occur to me how easily the law could have traced me after I passed the film in for processing in Lerwick some weeks later. However, it would have needed some punitive action on the part of the camera shop staff which, happily, they did not take.

The snapshot, when I eventually received it, clearly showed the deep slash of red stretching from under the beak almost to the gullet. The distinctive marking seemed to be a handicap to concealment of the otherwise rather drab grey bird, particularly as it had made no attempt to hide but had sat upright, showing off its fine feathers. If a weasel or stoat were its natural enemies, it was no mystery to me why this lovely bird was threatened with extinction.

Collecting my paper from the shop that evening, I asked Peerie Jessie who my trow was – identifying him by his red mini.

"That's Bertie Burnside," she said. "He lives oot past you. Da last hoose towards Otter's Dale. He's really Bertie Svenson. He cam here with da 'Shetland Bus' as a refugee during da war. You'll have heard aboot thae goins on, nae doot?"

I told her I had read the book.

"Yus, yus. Weel, he married a local lass. She died a couple o' year ago, puir soul. Their bairns are married sooth, du keens, so he's all by hissel. You should look along oor Johnsmas Foy idda haa in twartree weeks. Bertie's a rare fiddler, especially when he's ta'en a dram or two."

I worked out 'twartree' as 'two or three' and felt quite pleased with myself. Yet, listening to Peerie Jessie dealing with other customers, I realised I had a long way to go. To my ear, there appeared to be no difference between 'Is du gotten pepper?' and 'Is du gotten da pepper?', yet the first secured them a condiment and the second the daily news. 'Saat' and 'saat fush' were much the same as elsewhere in Scotland, but 'smocks' were either pinafores or cigarettes, and 'smucks' were slippers. It was all very confusing.

I did not go to church the first Sunday, but I went the next. I must admit this was not from any predilection to piety on my part, but rather from a sense of obligation to the good shepherd, Lowrie Petersen, whom I met in the shop during the week. In his mild mannered way he said he had missed seeing me in the kirk – as though I was part of the furniture. I didn't have the heart to disappoint him a second time and judging by the smallness of the congregation, he needed all the support he could get.

The Rev Sheila didn't particularly inspire me. She seemed to be much too full of her newly gained theology to find the necessary humility to minister to a lost sheep like me. I could not help wondering what the real shepherd was making of her, then I remembered his remark at the funeral about not taking responsibility for the sermon. It was my guess he could have preached a more telling gospel himself. Not that I was in any way disappointed. The view from the side window was all the inspiration I needed. (I had chosen my seat with the thought in mind.)

The church was on a small elevation about half a mile or so from the pier. It commanded one of the best views in the village. I could see the Mootie Skerries (the islands I had seen indistinctly from my first shore-walk) out beyond North Hoose. Waves were breaking against them in flashes of white, like semaphored messages from a ship. It occurred to me these low-lying islands would be a shipping hazard in rough weather. I wondered if there was a light on them.

North of the pier and closer inshore was another island. It was an irregular shape and named Tushkar Island on my map. There was a small stone hut in the middle, said to have been built by a hermit who lived there in the 16th century. Legend had it his wife took exception to his growing a beard and banished him to the island. On windy days his white beard could be seen blowing out across the island like smoke from a fire.

When the hermit had eaten all the mussels off the accessible beaches, and the only remaining ones were in a tiny cove at the foot of a cliff, he used to anchor himself by tying the end of his beard round a rock then abseiling down the cliff face. He did this whenever he needed a feed, but one day he was careless and chose an unstable rock. It dislodged when he was halfway down and went crashing after him. His body was never found but the rock with the white beard attached is still on the beach – or so they say.

The inspiring view triggered a memory of another window in another church – two churches in fact. The first is at the head of Lake Tekapo in New Zealand. Behind the altar is a picture window with a glorious view across the lake to the snow-capped Southern Alps. It is one of those places bus tours stop for what they call 'photo opportunities'.

By coincidence the other church is at the same latitude as the Bruntisdale one (60 deg N.) but at the opposite side of the world. I had camped for several days beside a lake at Auke Bay in Alaska. At one end of the lake is the spectacular Mendelhall Glacier. A blue/green ice field that inches its way out of the mountains to end in a three hundred foot cliff above the lake. From time to time huge slices of the cliff break away to crash outwards, sending shockwaves down the lake.

Locals used to row their dinghies out to these ice-flows and hack large chunks off, which they then towed back to the shore. The party thing to do was to hollow out a bowl-shaped catchment in the top of your chunk of ice then pour your fruit punch in. The compacted ice was many times colder than the refrigerator alternative and lasted for hours – even days.

At the far end of the lake, over a mile away amongst a scattering of houses, was a wooden A-frame church strategically set to capture the spectacular view. Seeing the congregation gathering on a Sunday morning, I threw on a clean pair of jeans and a half-way decent T-shirt and strolled over to join them. I had a reason.

The day before, I had been collecting wild berries along the shore of the lake, blueberries, salmonberries and a fat, red, mulberry-like fruit the natives called huckleberries. With one-for-me-and-one-for-the-billy, I was thoroughly enjoying myself when a brown bear walked down the pathway towards me. I was scared witless, having heard one too many stories about these unpredictable creatures. I would have taken to my heels (which apparently is not a smart thing to do), but I was rooted to the spot with fear. The bear stopped when it saw me, giving me a 'what have we here' stare. I wondered if it knew the meaning of 'shoo' but I couldn't have uttered it if I tried.

After what seemed eternity (probably about thirty seconds), the rather mangy looking beast turned aside and went crashing through the undergrowth. I realised it was almost certainly after berries itself and unlikely to trouble me, however that thought did not occur to me until later. I decided to settle for what was in my billy and high-tailed it back to the safety of my campsite.

I don't remember saying a prayer of thanksgiving for my deliverance, but no doubt I subconsciously thought God had worked one of his mysterious wonders on my behalf, so I went to church.

As in the case of Reverend Sheila, the Alaskan minister failed to hold my attention. I may say he was at a greater disadvantage because behind him the entire lakeside end of the building was glass. The view up to the glacier was breathtaking. In reality the preacher didn't stand a chance. It was a case of 'I shall lift my eyes unto the hills ... ' and forget all else.

The Bruntisdale view might not have been as spectacular or awe-inspiring, but there was a gentle beauty about it that was more than visual. My soul needed no bidding to be still. Some might have termed it a religious experience. What is religion, after all, but a reaching out for something beyond ourselves. A recognition that the act of worship lifts us to new levels of consciousness, making us receptive to 'higher things' (whatever they might be). One thing was certain. I would not be the first to find inspiration in the view from that window.

Some months later I attended a Crusade in the village hall. It was an interesting experience. Shetlanders are wonderfully ecumenical. They will front up to whichever sect or denomination is holding a revival or whatever and enthusiastically embrace the cause – for the duration of the event, that is. At all other times they are strictly Church of Scotland, barring maybe five per cent, who are indulgently accepted as eccentric.

The Salvation Church of the Assemblies of God came to Bruntisdale. All one-hundred-and-twenty-three residents and a black cat attended and sang the gospel hymns with commendable fervour ... well, the cat didn't sing, but it showed every inclination of being thoroughly appreciative of the experience, parading between the pews with its tail in the air.

The message was simple enough. We must all embrace the gospel, repent and be saved. According to the speaker – a roly-poly fellow with a shiny face – a true manifestation of our acceptance by God would result in our speaking in tongues. This achieved, the speaker would baptise us by total immersion (a portable swimming pool had been brought along for the purpose). We were assured God would receive us into his bosom, but only after we descended into the water – neck and crop, if you please.

The Biblical precedent for this, we were told, was the passing of the Children of Israel through the Red Sea. Excuse me! Wasn't that on dry land? I thought it was the Egyptians who got doused! Of course I kept my thoughts to myself. I am a bit of a coward in the face of holy zeal.

No-one actually converted to the Assemblies of God that evening, but a good time was had by all. No doubt the revivalist chalked it up as a successful meeting. Perhaps he had high hopes for the cat. Fat chance. Weren't cats sacred to the ancient Egyptians? Reincarnations of past Pharaohs, or some such? Certainly not amenable to total immersion, even in milk.

Chapter Four

The loch below my house was called Deep Loch. I took my rod one evening and walked down. It had been yet another of those misty days. Not cold, but a patch of blue would have been a nice change. I got my wish after tea, which is partly why I set off. I had been inside all day and my head was duffy.

Not that there was much blue sky. Enough to make a sailor's pair of trousers, as my grandmother used to say. And that was supposed to be the harbinger of fine weather to come. A bit of overcast is better for fishing in any case. Trout are shy fish and the open waters of the Shetland lochs make the angler's job all the harder. I have fished in many parts of the world and would have to say the Shetland inland waters are amongst the most challenging. The sea fishing is another story but I'll come to that later.

I generally like to tie my own flies and had brought the means to do so with me to Shetland. Once I discovered what the fish were feeding on I would adapt accordingly. The contents of a trout's stomach can tell you most of what you need to know. But first you have to catch one. Deep Loch looked like a good place to start.

The water lived up to its name, so I was able to fish from the bank, staying well back and casting into the shadows along the edge. A dry fly was called for as the trout were rising enthusiastically, sometimes jumping clear of the water.

I selected a brown dun which had a whisker of white in the tail. It was a good choice. I caught two half-pounders in rapid succession. After that it went quiet. A couple of half-hearted swirls then no more movement. There is no accounting for the whims of trout. I changed flies several times, trying both wet and dry, but they were having none of it.

The adrenalin rush of the catch had worn off. I was content to enjoy the evening light. The murmur of the sea just over the hill from me had a soporific effect. I sat a while, watching the soft movements of the breeze on the loch. The patterns of gold and crimson light, reflections of the simmer dim. Ever changing images in a kaleidoscope. Now broad bands, placid, lucid, luminescent. Now combed out to long streaks, before being strewn about in shards of colour like tumbled gems from a king's ransom.

This, I thought, was the 'magic of Shetland' promised me in the advertisement for Westerfield. I wished the peace and beauty might be everlasting. I supposed it could, but only in the loch. All else would change.

North Sea oil was beginning to flow in to Shetland, bringing with it all the hype and stress of big business. Already in Lerwick I had witnessed some of the attitudes I was used to in Edinburgh and elsewhere. No more the friendly, personalised service of bygone days. Now you waited in a queue, like as not to be confronted with a 'gone to lunch' sign at the end of it. Soon there would be litter in the streets, graffiti on walls and harassed looks on the faces of passers-by. Next would come drugs and despair – the things that destroyed a peaceful society. Everything would become disconnected and chaotic. The trouble was, unlike my loch, once broken, the picture would never return to the way it used to be. But I was being negative. Why spoil the magic.

(Of course there is always the danger of being naive about these things. Twenty years later my thoughts returned to haunt me. I wondered then, if Deep Loch still reflected an ideal world. The coming of oil created an economic boom in the islands such as had hitherto only been dreamed of, but it came at a price. The risk to the environment was, and is extreme, notwithstanding all that modern technology has devised to protect it. The doom and gloom merchants said it was a disaster waiting to happen. They were to be proved right.

A storm in 1993 drove the oil tanker Braer onto rocks near Sumburgh Head. The tonnage of lost crude oil equated with some of the worst accidental spills in history. The decimation of Shetland's unique bird life seemed inevitable. Indeed, the damage was considerable. Yet, by a quirk of nature, the wreck was so placed as to be largely influenced by favourable currents which, coupled with a wind change, carried the bulk of the oil spill far out to sea where it was broken up and dispersed. It could have been so much worse. The end effect saw even greater safeguards put in place. But Murphy's Law cannot be thwarted. If something can go wrong, it will. It is simply a matter of time.

Apparently there are no pristine regions left on earth. We have turned up man-made contaminants in the air at the South Pole. Most of our rivers and lakes are dying. Salination of our cropping lands is rampant and global warming is raising the level of the oceans. The so-called low counties of Holland are getting lower and presumably the Venetians will soon be wearing wellington boots to go about their daily business. It does not augur well for the future.

Perhaps I should have endeavoured to incorporate some sort of moral anecdote into my novel – like Aesop's Tales. But I lack the finesse. I am afraid I would wield the pen like a club rather than a sword.)

I had to pass close to a croft house on my way home. As I did so, a man came to the door and hailed me. He must have been watching my progress, probably with binoculars, like Old Bobby. I had noticed there seemed to be a pair handy in every house I visited.

"Any luck?"

I held up my catch to be admired. He was standing in shadow at the door so at first I did not recognise him. Now I could see it was Lowrie Petersen.

"Come away in," he said. "We're just aboot to hae wir eight-o'clocks. Du'll no refuse a cup o' tae."

As if I would.

I thanked him and kicked off my boots at the door. The sitting room was warm and friendly with a peat fire burning quietly in the gable end. The house had been sited to capture the view of both loch and sea, and the usual small, deeply recessed window, had been replaced with a four-by-two-foot picture one.

Along the coast to the south, the lights of the pierhouse and shop were already showing in the gathering twilight. The binoculars were on the sill. There would be little of the comings and goings of Bruntisdale missed by Lowrie.

Mrs Petersen came through from the but end of the house with a tray. Judging by the speed at which it was delivered, I could only assume she had made up a plate for me when I was still climbing the stile below the house.

"This is Maggie," Lowrie said.

She smiled. "Do you tak mylk, Mr Graham?"

"Please. And it's Stuart."

"She's fae Whalsay," Lowrie added, as though apologising for an indiscretion on his part. It probably explained her unusual pronunciation of 'milk'.

We were soon chatting like old friends. Shetlanders are like that. Once they take you to their hearts, you become one of the family. There is nothing contrived about this, it is simply a natural outcome of their generosity of spirit. Once the initial shyness or caution is overcome, it is as if they want to make up for appearing not to have trusted you in the first place. Their kindnesses can be overwhelming at times and you need not imagine you will ever be able to repay them for they will always outdo you in this regard.

Having lost my mother when I was seven, I have always been vulnerable to 'mothering'. Maggie Petersen seemed to recognise this need in me and made it her business to adopt the role. She must have been seventy-five, yet she made light of climbing the half mile to my house with a pie she had made especially for me, or a duck-egg sponge cake, or some other treat.

On one occasion she came with a beautiful Fair Isle jumper. A perfect fit, knitted in all the natural shades of undyed wool. When I protested such a generous present, she dismissed it with, "Och, it's nothin' at all. You'd likely get much better in Lerwick." But of course I wouldn't. The extra thought and care that was put into something knitted with love, made this sort of gift unique.

On that first evening (one of many) in the Petersen's home, I learned something of the tragedy which they had had to come to terms with in their lives. I had expressed an interest in exploring the headland beyond their home, having noted on my map the rocks and islands beyond. It looked like a place where I might obtain some interesting photography.

Maggie immediately became quite agitated at my mention of the place, wringing her hands and chewing her lower lip.

"It's a bad place ... " she began, but Lowrie cut in.

"Noo, noo, Maggie, du's no tae bother Stuart wi' yun."

I glanced from one to the other, saying nothing.

"Du'll tak a grain mair tae," Lowrie said, taking my cup and handing it to Maggie. It was clear he was more interested in diverting his wife than in dispensing hospitality. But the old lady was not to be denied. When she handed me back the filled cup, she bent her white head to me and said quietly, "We lost wir only son ower yun cliffs."

I think I had half suspected it must be something of the sort, but it came as a shock nonetheless.

Though Lowrie tried again to stop her talking, her mind was set. "Na, it's better that he sud keen." And she sat down, calm and composed now, with her hands folded in her lap.

Lowrie caught my eye and shook his head sadly, but he allowed his wife to tell her tale.

James Magnus was his name – except that Maggie spoke of him as Jeemsie Magnie. Shetlanders love to use the diminutive. It makes everything seem more precious somehow. He was only fifteen. It was the day after his birthday. A fine day, calm and sunny. Jeemsie Magnie had gone looking for gulls' eggs for his mother. Maggie liked to use them for making pancakes, believing they made a lighter batter than hens' eggs. "It's just a stupid notion I had," she said, obviously blaming herself for what had happened.

No-one knew the exact ins and outs of it, but the boy must have climbed down the cliff to get to a narrow ledge. They found his basket there. He had fallen, clutching desperately at outcrops and tufts of grass on the way down. The lacerations to his hands told that tale. By some freak of chance the fall had not killed him though he sustained serious internal injuries and multiple fractures.

The tide had been out at the time and Jeemsie Magnie had managed to drag himself into a cave. It was a fatal decision. The searchers on the cliff top found no clues apart from the basket, so the decision was taken to send a boatload of men to comb the beach. By the time they reached the right place it was high tide. Jeemsie Magnie had chosen the worst possible cave – one that filled with the tide. When the men found him he had already drowned.

"And to think," Maggie concluded, "he was taken by the sea when he should have been killed."

It was a weird notion, the significance of which escaped me, though I supposed it meant something to her.

Without a doubt the sea is the greatest danger to a people who largely depend on it for their livelihood. So many Shetlanders lost their lives as merchant seaman during both wars and every village has its fishermen who do daily battle with this, the most fickle of the elements. But the cliffs are dangerous too, especially to foolhardy youngsters and over-enthusiastic birdwatchers.

I did eventually go to that headland, visiting the graveyard on the way, where I found the lovingly tended plot of James Magnus Petersen '*Taken by the sea*'. The view from the cliffs was as spectacular as I had thought it would be. Only a narrow sea passage separated the Noss from the mainland with several giant rocks between them, all white with guano.

There must have been thousands of sea birds wheeling about between the cliffs and rocks. I recognised guillemots, kittiwakes, skuas, Atlantic gulls, terns and the comical little puffins (that went by the delightful Shetland name of 'tammie norrie'), skimming and swooping as they propelled their fat little bodies on seemingly inadequate wings in a frenzy of flapping. By comparison, fulmar petrels glided effortlessly on the updraught, floating to within an arms-length of my face, turning quizzical heads to study me as they drifted past.

Far below, on the rocks and in the sea surrounding them, I could make out a colony of seals. Here and there orange buoys marked lobster pots. I didn't fancy the idea of taking a boat in there to retrieve them. It would want a calm day and the slack of the tide.

I remembered this was supposed to be the scene of the shipwreck Young Bobby had told me about. The place might be expected to have had a haunted feel about it, but I must admit it did not strike me in this way. The abundant bird life seemed so raucously exuberant, the air so like champagne, and the sea so sparklingly bright, I felt light-headed and light-hearted.

One day, on the way to the shop, I determined to call Old Bobby's bluff. He was bent over his carving, paying me no heed as I approached, though I knew full well he must be aware of my presence. An old whaler like Bobby (for that was what he was), who could detect a sail on the horizon in a storm or the spout of a whale before sun-up, would hardly miss the likes of me at twenty paces.

I bade him good day and got his usual "harrumph" in reply. He might have been a beached walrus, which, in a way he was.

"Can I take a look?" I asked pointing to his work. He held it out to me in gnarled old hands that looked like eagle's talons. I was surprised to discover it was whalebone and not driftwood as I had thought. Old Bobby was actually engaged in the ancient art of scrimshaw, intricately etching a schooner in full rig. In the foreground was a longboat, oars dipped and men straining backwards against them. A figure in the stern was pointing over their heads towards the spout of a whale. There was so much vitality in the work you could almost hear the shout of "Thar she blows!"

I had seen similar pieces in the Maritime Museum in Edinburgh but had thought it a lost art. I was genuinely awestruck.

"This is a fantastic piece of work, Bobby," I said in fulsome praise.

"I've better ones inside." He might have been a merchant admitting to having offered me an inferior tin of ship's biscuits.

"Can I see them?"

He took his hat off and scratched his head. (His eyes were green.) It was obviously a matter of some consequence to him. If he gave way now he would have to concede the battle of wits.

"If you like," he said at length and levered himself up off the bench.

The pierhouse must have been very old. It was built of roughly cut bluestone with solid doors and window-frames in Baltic pine. It was the largest building in Bruntisdale, measuring about 40 by 90 feet. The three floors were supported by timber pillars across which lay heavy beams, all adze-trimmed and bolted together.

The top floor was unpartitioned, making it ideal for wedding receptions and dances in the early days before the village hall was built. The second floor had served as warehousing in the days when Bruntisdale had been a herring curing station of some repute. Bags of salt and empty barrels had been swung up here on the gantries at the front of the building to await the start of the season.

Later it had stored all manner of produce for the village – bags of wool and potatoes, coils of rope, salvaged timber from the beach, stock-feed, sacks of flour, roofing iron. Anything and everything passed through the pierhouse at one time or another, including the occasional keg of brandy or rum that had made its way by devious means to Seal

Bay. A sizeable winch, bolted to the floor adjacent to one of the gantries, made light work of the more cumbersome items.

Originally the pierhouse had belonged to the laird of Bruntisdale who, it was said, once confiscated a crofter's pig and hauled it up to the second floor where he threatened to butcher it if the unfortunate tenant did not pay his rent. Old Bobby was supposedly a distant relative of the present laird who now lived in exile in Canada, collecting his meagre purse of rental from the ever-dwindling crofters.

The ground floor was Old Bobby's domain, though in reality he used only two rooms of it. His bathroom was a converted stable at the back with a large tin bath standing in the middle of the floor. Old Bobby kept his potatoes in the bath where he believed the mice could not nibble at them. But he had not reckoned on the disconnected plug hole. In a season of meagre supply, the mice swarmed in from below and ate their way upwards. By the time Bobby discovered the thieves, they had ruined half his winter's store.

Bobby's living quarters were a cornucopia of accumulations from a lifetime of travel. He had sailed 'further than Sinbad', as he liked to put it, having started out as a twelve-year-old on a whaler. As I glanced round the room I very quickly discovered scrimshaw was his chief delight. Apart from many items of his own work, which he proceeded to show me with some pride, he also had a sizeable collection of unusual pieces he had picked up along the way. To my untrained eye, Bobby's own work was every bit as good as the best of the others.

All his items were on nautical themes, worked on whale's teeth mainly, but also on walrus tusks and even old ivory piano keys. My favourite was of a tousle-headed boy sitting on a quayside bolster beside an old salt (who might have been Bobby himself judging by the cap and roll-neck jumper). The boy was plucking the old man's sleeve to get a turn at the spy-glass with which the old fellow was studying a sail on the horizon. The cameo had captured the feeling of pent up excitement in the youngster together with the 'when I'm good and ready' attitude of the man. It had been worked on a superior specimen of unflawed, honey-toned whale's tooth. I'd have given my own eye teeth for it.

Having broken down the barrier between us, as it were, Bobby now became the soul of geniality towards me. Whenever I passed his bench he would give it a pat and say, "Dip dee aside me for a peerie start," meaning me to sit down a moment for a chat. More frequently than not it was a half hour or so, for the old fellow was full of tales. I discovered to my surprise he was 90 years old, yet he still worked his intricate etchings without the aid of glasses.

He told me stories of the Cape region, South Georgia, and all places between. He seemed to have spent half his life in the roaring forties. Some of his tales had me on the edge of the seat, yet when I came to jot them down later the bare words seemed fanciful in the extreme. It needed Bobby's telling to give them the ring of truth.

Once, after provisioning in Hobart, the crew had thought to explore the region around Macquarie Island, south of Tasmania. It was in the early 20s when whales were becoming scarce on the traditional grounds near South Georgia. Passing below the Maatsuyker light, the ship had come near a small uncharted island and the lookout had sighted a flag. They had put a boat ashore and found a pathetically emaciated Russian, who, in broken English, told them he had been stranded alone for over a month.

His ship had gone down off King Island in the Bass Strait, he and five others getting off in a lifeboat. They had been carried southwards past Three Hummocks Island and on down the west coast of Tasmania. Though they were in sight of land most of the time, the winds held them off despite every effort they made. The emergency rations had been tampered with leaving provisions for less than a week. It was a major blow. They soon became weak and dispirited.

After eight days of battling heavy seas and constant rain, the boat had passed round the south-west tip of Tasmania and been driven out of sight of land for the first time. The food was gone and all were suffering from exposure, hypothermia and starvation. They believed themselves beyond hope.

In the following days four of the seamen died. The Russian and his remaining companion had no option but to heave the bodies overboard. The lighter the boat, the better their chances of survival, though survival was no longer a prospect they discussed.

The two men endured another four days in a state of semi-delirium. Then one night they saw a light. The Russian's mate said it was the angel Gabriel coming for them, but they soon concluded it was a lighthouse. When dawn came they had hoped to see land but the ocean was empty. To the west another storm was brewing. Lightning flashes lit up the horizon and thunder reverberated around them. The men lay down in the bottom of the boat. Death would be a welcome release.

But they did not die. In that vast expanse of empty sea, the boat found a tiny island and bumped gently ashore before the storm broke. Somehow they struggled out, yet were too weak and delirious to think of securing the boat. They found shelter under an overhanging rock shelf and survived the storm. Next morning the boat was gone.

Then began a second nightmare of survival. There were mutton birds (shearwaters) on the island which the men dragged out of their burrows before clubbing them to death and eating the raw flesh. It proved to be surprisingly nourishing. They became stronger.

Each day they wandered the tiny island looking for alternative sustenance. As it rained more often than not, there was no shortage of fresh water. Each night they returned to their rock ledge shelter. After a week had passed (during which they supplemented their diet with shellfish and seaweed), they saw a ship passing to their north. They ran round the island waving frantically but the vessel continued on its course, passing out of sight to the north-east. That night they sat at the northern extremity of their island, watching the point at which the ship had vanished, willing it to come back.

It was then they saw the lighthouse again. The sequence of flashes was the same as before. It appeared to be quite close – perhaps three miles away. In great excitement they climbed to the highest vantage point at first light and could just make out land. Another island, they thought, or a headland. So near and yet so far. It was the worst torment of all.

Three days later the Russian's companion was bitten by a snake. He had put his hand down a mutton bird burrow and grabbed the snake instead. It was a tiger snake, one of the world's most venomous reptiles. The man was dead within five hours. The Russian had sat holding the dead man's body all night. In the morning he dug a shallow grave in the sandy soil and buried him.

Nearly five more desperate weeks were to pass before Old Bobby's whaler hove into sight. The Russian had thought he would go insane but whenever the weather permitted, he sat and watched the lighthouse flashing. It came to be a symbol for him, a promise of salvation. The light was obviously there for a purpose. He was in a region where shipping passed frequently enough to warrant a lighthouse. A ship would come. He never gave up hope.

The captain of the whaler offered to put the Russian ashore at Maatsuyker Island but he chose to sign on and travel with them to the whaling. After all, he said, he was a seaman.

Chapter Five

I had been in Bruntisdale nearly three weeks before I met Jessie and Bobby's two sons. They were both in their teens and attended the Anderson Institute in Lerwick where they boarded during the week. The elder, James, took me to Otter's Dale late one evening in the hope of sighting an otter. He said they often played at the mouth of Brat Burn. We lay on the hillside for nearly an hour, scanning the scene with binoculars but were out of luck. Later in the year I saw otters at both Brat Burn and below Deep Loch.

The Shetland name for these delightful creatures is 'dratsie', apparently a descriptive term for their rather drunken walk. Their element is clearly the sea, where they move with such fluidity as to seem part of the very waves they love to surf and tumble in. On land they are more furtive, moving swiftly across the ground in a slightly disjointed gait, glancing nervously from side to side.

Their burrows, where they rear their young, are usually close to water. To find one, however, calls for great patience and keen eyes as the otter will wait for dusk to come ashore then move in short bursts, doubling back and disappearing under banks to re-emerge where least expected.

They like the cover of a burn to travel inland, diving into pools, then surfacing alongside rocks or overhanging vegetation such as marsh-marigolds. The only sign of their passing may be the telltale movement of grass as they hug the ground, out of sight.

The reason we saw nothing that first night may well have been because James was such a chatterbox. He was a natural story-teller, like his father, full of improbable tales and folklore. To hear him tell it, no-one in the village was normal. They all had weird afflictions, eccentricities or dark secrets. Bertie Burnside was actually a Russian spy. You could see his light come on at 2am every morning when he sent coded short-wave messages to the Kremlin about North Sea oil shipping movements.

Charlie Groat, who lived in the house below the hall, ate nothing but McVitie's Cream Crackers and peanut butter. He had more sheep than anyone else and spent most of his time wandering the hills checking up on them. Whenever he sighted an unmarked one, he sent Jess, his collie, to run it down, then earmarked it with his own insignia and added it to his flock.

Elsie the Loch had a cellar under her house stacked with bottles of French brandy, which her father had smuggled ashore over 80 years before. He had been drowned bringing in the last boatload. Everyone knew the grog was there because Elsie brought a bottle to the Church Fair once. The minister refused to put it up for auction, confiscating it instead. The next day he rode his bicycle off the end of the pier and had to be hauled out by Peter Poulson who was fishing there at the time.

Charlie Green, the postman, had a house full of cats. He picked up strays, carrying them home in a fishing creel on the back of his motorbike. Why he kept them was a mystery because he became extremely bad-tempered when they tripped him up, roaring his stock-in-trade, "I'll shaw dee da toun o' Bruntisdale upside doon," and raising his boot to give substance to the threat. Whether any of his moggies had actually taken the journey was a matter for conjecture.

By the time James ran out of stories and fell silent, the night had closed in around us and we were more likely to see a trow than an otter.

Back at home Peerie Jessie told me an amusing story about James. When Old Bobby retired and came home to live in the pierhouse, a certain amount of work had to be done to make it habitable. It had been closed up for years. Even the windows were boarded up to prevent mischievous boys from breaking them. It had never been wired for electricity and the plumbing was in a parlous state.

The Smiths offered Old Bobby a room until the place was made ready for him. It took two months. In the meantime the old man proved to be a bit of a handful. He was restless to begin with, chaffing at the hawser of rheumy bones which now kept him moored against his will.

He could not sit still; forever getting up out of his chair to wander out thc back door, re-entering minutes later at the front. He would sit a while, then repeat the process. Peerie Jessie wearied of closing doors behind him, for *he* never did. One door was a nuisance, two meant a whistling draught.

One day, when Jessie was busy baking and four-year-old James was sitting on a high stool watching television, Old Bobby began his wandering.

"James, be a peerie darlin' and shut that door for Mam."

It was something of an effort for the child to get down off the stool to do his mother's bidding, but he did it with good grace. The second time he was less enthusiastic and the third time downright rebellious.

"Please," his mother pleaded.

James, looking daggers at his mother, ran to both doors and keyed them. "Noo da ould booger can tak anither gait an' I can watch *The Magic Roundabout* in paece!" According to Jessie she had to stick her head in a cupboard to hide her laughter.

I heard many a tale of the sea and fisherfolk from Tom Renwick. He would invite me aboard his trawler at the end of the day "for a dram and a chew of the rag" to use his expression. He told me of the Haaf, which had been the principal method of catching fish up until fifty years hence. Six and eight-oared custom-made boats were manned by men whose livelihood depended on their skill in rowing the boats up to thirty miles offshore where the best fishing grounds were.

It was a dangerous occupation with virtually every household having its own tale of tragedy to tell. As it was always the best of the able-bodied men who were lost, many a croft lived out a generation with only women and children having to fend for themselves.

Once, after a couple of drams, Tom broke into song.

Oot bewast the Horn o' Papa
Rowin Foula doon!

(*Mair Laeves Fae Vagaland*;
T. A. Robertson, The Shetland Times, 1965.)

It was a rollicking tune that had the lumpy sea in its rhythm; Tom's powerful baritone set to carry far across the water. He explained the sentiment of the lyrics to me, which told something of the romance of the haaf fishing. It was not unusual for the boats to be caught out in a sea-mist with visibility down to zero. Yet they could 'row Foula doon' on the scent of the summer flowers. Knowing how the scent of thrift carried from the cliff tops, it seemed entirely plausible to me.

According to Tom, there was scarcely a geo, skerry or headland in Shetland that did not have a tale of misfortune or shipwreck attached to it. I heard again the story of the shipwrecked Irish boy (with Tom's original embellishments), and many more tales besides.

"Da Russian trawler skippers aye get dir charts upside-doon and geng da wrang side o' da lighthooses," he claimed. "There was one gaed on da Sooth Ness, ootby du keens, twartree year ago. All hands were lost. I mind, a body cam ashore two weeks later – weel, just da trunk, du keens, all ravaged by da sea."

"There's a great oncarry divin' amang da wrecks," he began on another occasion.

"You mean fortune hunters?" I asked.

"Yus yus, and all yun clubs wi dir historical palaver and da liks. Shoals o' dem come up in da simmer, lik da fishes."

I smiled at the notion of the seabed being congested with aqualungs.

Tom reckoned there were several of the Spanish Armada galleons sunk around Shetland: "Wi' loads o' dragoons on board."

"Doubloons," I ventured.

"Exactly." Tom wasn't about to admit a slip of the tongue.

He had little respect for what he called the 'weekend sailors'. "Worse than Sunday drivers," he claimed. "They tak a yacht oot in a half-gale, then expect us to pull them oot o' da sea when they're dismasted. And it's little thanks du gets for dee trouble," he added with feeling.

"It's fine to tak a dram, pierside," he opined. "But whisky and saat watter's a bad mix."

It seemed Tom had had more than his share of troublesome rescues.

Sometimes, if Greta was in Lerwick shopping and not expected home till late, Tom cooked us a fish supper in his orderly galley. Once we stayed because "Greta's in a mood." I asked no questions. Tom was a better cook than I was. No sense rocking the boat.

I learned of the extraordinary superstitions of a fisherman. Cats, in particular, were apparently a bad omen. Meeting one on the way to his boat was enough reason to abort an outing. Even to mention the word was bad luck. No fisherman went to sea on Sunday though many started their week at a minute past midnight.

When James Smith and I were sitting on the slopes of Otter's Dale, he had pointed out a dilapidated house across the road from Bertie Burnside's. James told me it was called 'The Bogs' and belonged to twin sisters Maggie and Brenda Kellson who were in their late 80s. He said they were witches. Who was I to doubt it.

I often saw Maggie on the road and once made the mistake of offering her a lift. Apparently the sisters used their bath for storing peats. It explained a lot. You very quickly learned not to stand downwind of Maggie. Brenda apparently never left the house, which was probably just as well.

Maggie walked the three miles to the shop every other day for bread and cheese, procrastinating endlessly on whether or not to buy tea as well. She always decided against it with an audible sigh. One day Peerie Jessie gave her a packet, knowing full well what the outcome would be. The next day Maggie returned it, saying Brenda told her to. She did not elaborate further.

Jessie explained to me that Brenda made her own tea out of dried dandelions and seaweed. Maggie loathed the stuff, longing for a cup of Robur which her mother used to buy. But she was too simple-minded to take matters into her own hands.

James' younger brother, Davie, was a bit of a tearaway. He was only fourteen but had already been in the hands of the police for being drunk and disorderly on the streets of Lerwick. Half his problem was boredom. He was very intelligent and was unchallenged by school. He seldom came home at weekends, preferring the bright lights of the town – not that there were many bright lights in Lerwick. He was clearly a great worry to his mother.

I would have liked to help but it was none of my business. In any case there would have been little I could do. I am not a qualified counsellor and he was unlikely to accept advice from an interfering 'sooth moother'. Then I hit on an idea. Young Bobby had mentioned Davie's favourite pastime was going to the eela. This was a form of sea fishing in which rods with fixed lengths of line are used.

The problem was that Bobby never seemed to have time to take Davie. So, I persuaded Bobby to take *me*, then mentioned to Davie that we were going. He immediately asked to join us and there was no reason to refuse him. I could hardly tell Bobby he should try and spend more time with his son. This way I was able to bring about the same effect.

It turned out to be a most exciting experience. We each had two rods. We were fishing for coalfish – not very tasty, but a lot of fun. They had been pretty much fished out around Shetland but Bobby had a spot he knew of on the seaward side of Tushkar Island.

The trick was to row the boat into the middle of broken water where there was plenty of foam, then draw the lines through the water near the surface. The lures were small white feathers. The fixed lengths of line made it possible to swing a catch inboard without any adjustment. It was all go for a while. Very exciting. When we had more than enough fish and the novelty was wearing off, Bobby started the outboard and took us on down towards the mouth of the burn below Deep Loch. He reckoned salmon were sometimes to be had there.

I asked Davie if he had ever seen the rock on Tushkar Island with the hermit's hair tied to it.

"Lots of times," he said. But he failed to identify the spot. I supposed legend had to have its believers as well as its doubters if it was to survive.

It was a rare evening with all the sky and sea lit by the simmer dim. Arctic terns were flitting about like swallows, dipping suddenly to snatch at flashes of silver below the surface. What I would see as a trick of the light, they unerringly saw as a good catch. The Shetland name for the Arctic tern is 'tirrick' – a mimic of its call.

We drifted about at the mouth of the burn for a while. It was not as if we had any salmon-fishing gear with us, more the thought of being where they were, or might be. An odd notion, you might think, but there is no accounting for the mind of a fisherman. In any case, as far as I was concerned, the purpose of the exercise was being adequately realised. Father and son were spending time together.

In mid-June, Peerie Jessie reminded me about the foy which was to take place the next Saturday. In earlier days it had been celebrated as 'Simmermill', a pagan festival to mark midsummer's day. Since the coming of Christianity all the festivals had been taken over by the church and renamed for saints or sacred anniversaries like Hallowmas and indeed Christmas. Simmermill was now the Johnsmas Foy.

It started out as a sort of concert with everyone taking turns at the entertaining. Some recited poetry, others sang or played the fiddle. Charlie Green sang his item second on the programme. Apparently he always did, as he became too drunk later on. He sang 'Boots, boots, boots', raising a cloud of dust from the stage in his enthusiasm.

There was a short masked play with a good deal of ribald nonsense designed to send up all and sundry. Next, a small boy sang 'Annie's Song' to the accompaniment of the school band. When he got to "Come let me fill you, come fill me again," he forgot the next line. The band played on while he kept jumping in and out with catch-up lines, like a child in the playground trying to get in under the whirling skipping rope.

Every time the tune coincided with his particular needle in the groove, he would lustily sing "Come let me fill you, come fill me again," before returning to his stop/start staccato. The band seemed equally incapable of extricating itself, members looking daggers at the unfortunate singer. At the fourth " ... fill me again," Peter Poulson called out, "Lay off boy, I'se as full as a gus already."

"Du's said right der, Peter," Greta Renwick replied, having noted the slur in his speech. Mercifully some enterprising person took matters into their own hands, reaching from behind the curtain to snatch the boy off stage before he became as full as Peter. As entertainment, it earned the best applause of the night.

Between items there had been a good deal of surreptitious passing of hip flasks amongst the men who lounged about in the shadows at the back of the hall. As far as I was concerned it was a case of, "I don't mind if I do."

Supper was served at ten o'clock. Tattie soup, ham sandwiches, fancies and very strong tea poured out of enormous enamel teapots. Everyone was seated at long trestle tables which were covered with white butcher's paper.

After supper the floor was cleared then some patent white powder was sprinkled over the boards to make it slippery for dancing. The old folks took themselves off to bed, dragging sleepy but still reluctant toddlers with them. Everyone else came to life as the band struck up. From then on it was fast and furious.

Bertie Burnside played like one possessed, driving his bow across an open second string in a sort of accompanying drone to the melody. I had not heard fiddle playing like it before. Perhaps it had its origins in Norway. He had a tot of whisky at his elbow which was kept permanently totted. Every time he tossed it back the music was stepped up another gear.

The hip flasks must have been getting replenished from somewhere as they kept doing the rounds long after they might be expected to have run dry. More people began arriving – people I had never seen before. The place became as crowded as a cattle market and about as smelly. Even Maggie o' The Bogs would have felt quite at home in that company.

The dancing went on until 4am – or so I was told. I must admit the latter part of the night was a bit of a blur owing to the aforementioned hip flasks that kept passing my way. I remember dancing with a green-eyed vision, but had thought it was a dream. I don't remember how I got home.

I ended up attending several foys during my time in Bruntisdale. Just about anything became an excuse to hold one. In the bygone days they even had a 'Gude-keens Foy' for 'God only knows' what reason!

The biggest event on the calendar is Up-Helly-A'. It is a fire festival which celebrates (among other undefined things) the end of the winter solstice. With squads of Vikings, a torchlight procession, and the burning of a magnificent full size galley ship, it is a grandiose affair. Yet, despite the festival song's opening line (*From grand old Viking centuries, Up-Helly-A' has come*), the modern-day event bears little resemblance to the historical festival of that name.

Much of what takes place has no foundation in ancient custom. Not that anyone is unduly perturbed. The show has become a spectacle of such international standing as to attract at least two or three television crews every year. No sooner has one Up-Helly-A' finished, than the management committee starts planning the next – and building a new galley!

The main event is in Lerwick, but many country districts hold their own Up-Helly-A' festivals. Bruntisdale's centred around the pierhead with a small galley being towed down the pier on the fish trolley and hurriedly tipped over the end after it was put to the torch. It didn't make a lot of sense but then neither did most of the other foys. What mattered was the coming together of the community in a united effort designed to give enjoyment and entertainment to all.

Speaking of foys, the annual sheep-shearing had many elements of a good foy – or perhaps circus would be a better word. During the course of one of our conversations, I had been telling Lowrie Petersen about my stint on the sheep station in New Zealand, and how I had learned to make a passable job of shearing sheep. He immediately asked if I would like to come and help at the 'rooin'' in July. I said I didn't think I had actually ruined any sheep, at which he laughed heartily.

"Na, na. Rooin' is what we ca' shearin'. In da olden days it was a' rooin' but hit's mair shearin' noo."

I told him he had lost me, so he explained.

The Shetland sheep is small and hardy – hardy enough to be left in the hills during all but the worst winters. However, the extreme conditions and lack of feed causes the fleece to stop growing for a period. In the spring, when wool growth resumes, a distinct break forms between the old and the new. By June or July it is possible to pull away the old fleece without any injury or discomfort to the sheep. This is called rooing in Shetland. It is a rather wasteful process because the fleece tends to come away piecemeal as it catches in the heather. A crofter seeking to harvest his crop, as it were, will need to comb the hills with a bag over his shoulders. Indeed that was the common practise for centuries.

Modern day cross-breeding, together with improved husbandry, which includes provision for feed supplements and mineral licks, has largely eliminated the growth break, meaning the wool now grows continuously and has to be sheared. In 1975 in Bruntisdale, this meant hand clippers, although portable mechanical shears were becoming popular elsewhere in Shetland.

The day for the rooing was set for the first Saturday in July, weather permitting. The weather did permit and several crofters headed for the hills at daybreak to begin the muster.

I should explain, not all crofts had sheep out on the scattald. Over the years many men had found employment of other sorts and had relinquished their 'hill-rights' to other crofters. There were probably fewer than a dozen Bruntisdale crofts with sheep in the hill, though several more kept a few in what they called 'the park' or 'in-fields' close to the houses. These were kept mainly to fatten for fresh meat and for the ubiquitous reestit mutton.

To be precise, the muster had begun the day before, with two or three men going to the outer limits of the scattald to begin driving the sheep towards the pens at Sheep-dip Loch, which was more or less the centre of the district. Overnight these sheep did not stray far, so the muster resumed in the morning, with the circle being tightened.

By about ten o'clock, the rest of the village began to gather at Sheep-dip Loch to help with the final round-up. It was at this point the whole affair took on the appearance of a circus, largely due to there being too many over-excited dogs. There was a lot of whistling, flapping of arms, and waving of crooks. A lot of shouting: "Git du back der, Jess," or "Come du in, Rover," and "Git yun dug oot o' da grind (gate). Witna fule owns yun stupid cratur' onywey?"

In the midst of it all, the sheep (which were anything but domesticated, having spent the greater part of their lives more or less wild in the hills), were jumping over walls or running into the loch. Being sheep, fortunately they tended to follow the mob. Once a few had been coaxed into the pens, the rest soon followed and order was restored.

The dogs went and lay in the loch to cool off. The men took off their hats and jackets for much the same reason and began reassuring one another that they had had the whole affair under control from the start. "It's yun weemenfolk an' bairns. Dey aye get idda wey," seemed to be the consensus of opinion.

The shearing was very much a community affair with everyone giving a hand. Ownership was established by earmarks, with a good deal of surreptitious use of marking tools early on – especially by Charlie Groat who was an expert at it. I was told the clearskins were deemed to belong to the minister in earlier days. If so, he would have done quite well out of it. Not in 1975, however.

The drill seemed to be to tie the sheep's legs together then set to at the most convenient point. In many cases two people worked on the one animal, clipping down opposite sides. It was still possible to roo some of the sheep, or to partially do so. This job fell mainly to the women and children. The hill was soon scattered with bits of wool which the children ran around snatching up with squeals of delight.

Everyone was involved, clipping and chattering; stuffing fleece into all manner of brightly coloured plastic bags, then congregating around picnic baskets for thermos tea and bannocks. It was perhaps the last genuinely communal activity of a society that had at one time depended upon such co-operation for their very survival. As a spectacle, it beat the best of the foys hands down. I would not have missed it for anything.

My own estate had a Cheviot flock, so I knew a bit about wool. I had taken a special interest in the fine wool breeds of Australia and New Zealand and knew the significance of the various microns. I was also aware that the Shetland breed of sheep has unique characteristics which make it special. The combination of comparatively fine micron and exceptional insulating qualities make Shetland wool one of the world's best natural fibres. It may be something to do with the slightly hairy nature of the wool, coupled with the way the Scottish mills have perfected spinning of the yarn. Whatever it is, my mountaineering friend always maintained the most valuable item in his rucksack was a Shetland jumper.

"Its weight to warmth ratio is unsurpassable," he claimed.

Certainly Fair Isle knitting has made Shetland hosiery famous, but in my opinion, the wool is worthy of greater recognition in its own right.

In the midst of all my extra-curricular activities, I am sorry to say, my book was languishing. I had typed up a few pages of preamble but when I came to read them through they were more pre-ramble. The problem was I enjoyed fishing late into the night then slept in in the morning. The simmer dim was pure magic.

I noticed when the evening skies were at their best, everyone seemed to be out and about till all hours. There were few enough of these perfect days so no-one wanted to waste a minute of them. It might be eleven at night yet folks were strolling on the beach or taking a boat out. It was best to be near water because the reflected sky doubled the enjoyment.

For my part, even the rainy nights were still good for fishing – in fact they were better. I soon got to know the best spots and also narrowed down the choice of flies after dissecting my first few catches. The locals did not go much for 'da troots' and were amused at my persistence. Peter Poulson, who preferred the end of the pier, clearly thought I was mad.

"Wit wey's du wantin' tae gang plooterin' aboot in yun graet muckle buits win du cud be sittin' paeceable lik on a rock?" he asked.

But I went on 'plooterin' and my writing suffered. I consoled myself with the thought that the days would soon draw in and December was a long way away. There would be plenty time for writing in the autumn.

Chapter Six

I wished Peerie Jessie would stock the occasional lettuce or broccoli and told her so one day. If I kept going on the way I was, scurvy might well become an issue.

"Du's gotten a kaleyird," she said. "What's keepin' dee fae growin' dee own?"

I had to admit she had a point. I went home and surveyed my patch of nettles.

It took the best part of a day with an old garden fork I found in the barn. The soil looked good. It ought to, with heavens knew how many years of being fortified by the winter's accumulations from the byre. If it could produce such a noble crop of nettles and dockens, it could surely take care of a row or two of peas. I knew it would have been better to plant earlier but there was still time to bring on a crop.

I ordered some lettuce, cauliflower and broccoli plants from Lerwick, to be brought out with the mail car. Peerie Jessie had packets of carrot seed and peas for sale. I even got a couple of strawberry plants from Greta and a rhubarb crown from Charlie Green, after he had wandered through the cottage and out the back door in search of me to deliver the plants. I decided to put the strawberries in pots in my front porch and brought on some lettuces the same way. It was a case of hedging my bets.

The problem with the garden, as with all gardens in Shetland, was the wind. The walling helped, but a gale from the wrong direction could find its way in and wreak havoc. It seemed the wind liked to have the upper hand. All in all I had modest success. Scurvy was averted for the time being.

With the garden now taking care of itself, I turned my attention to some serious writing. It was make or break time. Either I must show some results or pack my bags. At least, that is what I told myself. The next three weeks saw a flurry of creative activity in the but end of Westerfield. Pages of script flowed out of my typewriter (even if most of them ended up in tightly screwed balls under the table). I had never imagined it would be so hard. It was a lonely, frustrating time. Yet I was determined to have something to show for my work.

I think I tried too hard. Either that, or the excessive amount of coffee was addling my brain. I ceased to be objective. I was now writing for the sake of writing. Heading for a black hole of antimatter.

Young Bobby saved me from self-destruction. He turned up one morning in his van.

"I'm off tae Scallowa' wi' a load o' fish. Fancy a run? I've got to go on tae Lerwick, so du can dae da tourist bit if du's wantin'."

I looked at the mess around me, trying to make some sense out of it.

"Come on," Bobby said. "Du's been cooped up in here for weeks. Jessie's been worried aboot dee."

"Yeah. I've been worried about me too. Okay, just let me grab my camera and I'll be with you."

It was one of those indifferent sorts of days that make up the bulk of Shetland's weather. You know – days when it is difficult to tell where the sky ends and the hills begin.

Not that it mattered. Bobby was a great conversationalist and in any case I was all but asphyxiated by the smell of fish.

Scalloway was the ancient capital of Shetland. Just a few streets really, around a sheltered harbour. This was where the 'Shetland Bus' had secretly operated from throughout the war.

A number of small wooden fishing boats that risked the North Sea and the German naval machine to bring refugees out of Norway and return with agents and saboteurs. It was a daring and audacious exercise that earned the admiration of all who knew about it. Not many did. It was one of the war's best kept secrets.

Scalloway harbour and waterfront appeared cluttered and in desperate need of some town-planning. Attractive but disused old warehouses in quarried stone stood cheek by jowl with ugly modern buildings, the latter bustling with activity. The streets were too narrow and congested with lorries and vans.

In the midst of the chaos stood Earl Patrick's castle, built in 1600. Like the earl, the castle had lost its head and now seemed to symbolise the general feeling of decay in the town.

Once we had unloaded our cargo and were headed for Lerwick with the windows down, things got better.

I had only been in Lerwick a couple of times so it was still a novelty. We came in past a loch with a well-preserved broch in the centre. The housing in this part of town was a mixture of dinky modern bungalows and older semi-detached dwellings in grey harled brick. Typical Scottish suburbia on a small scale. Nothing to write home about. Then again, the broch was pretty impressive, given that it was an Iron Age fort or dwelling of some sort. In fact, judging by the standard of some of the modern dwellings, I'd say we had regressed in the ensuing couple of thousand years.

The older part of town encompassed the harbour and the steep hill overlooking it. This was more interesting; much more interesting. Narrow winding lanes, many of them made up of steps, connected the hilltop with the waterfront. The area was part residential, part commercial, with fascinating little shops tucked away in corners and individually styled houses with quaint angles. Bright pot plants on balconies and terraces added a splash of colour to an otherwise grey scene.

Many of the buildings were of undressed bluestone and the streets and lanes were flagged or cobbled with the same material. The town's main street was immediately adjacent to the wharf area. It was more a lane than a street, which turned at right angles as it passed between the jutting-out buildings. In several places there was width enough for only one car.

Some of the buildings were over four storeys high which meant very little light made its way down to the cobbles. It would not be a place to hurry on a wet day. For the moment, however, the shafted sunlight accentuated the angles and inspired the photographer in me. Although it was officially titled 'Commercial Street' it was known throughout Shetland as 'da street'. It was the place to meet friends when you went to town. It encompassed two hotels, most of the old established business houses, all the banks and a market cross.

At the southern extremity of the town were the 'lodberries' – houses with their foundations below the tide line. It was this part which earned Lerwick its tourist label of 'The Venice of the North'. Beyond the lodberries, a headland known as the Knab, was a popular vantage point from which to watch the *St Clair* sail out 'da sooth mooth' between the mainland and the isle of Bressay on its tri-weekly voyage to Aberdeen. From here you could also see the 'klondykers' – Russian fish-factory ships – surrounded by a perpetual squall of gulls. Their supply trawlers worked outside the seven-mile limit, dredging the sea at an alarming rate.

Young Bobby and I had gone our separate ways on arrival in the town, agreeing to meet at Da Noost for lunch. Da Noost was the favoured meeting place amongst out-of-town day-shoppers. I especially liked their crumbed haddock and chips. The decor was unpretentious, the service cheery and homely, and the gossip at neighbouring tables made for good eavesdropping.

"Is du gyaan tae da unction?" I heard an elderly woman ask her table companion.

I thought it must be some sort of Catholic blessing and asked Young Bobby about it. He nearly choked on his fish. "Na, na," he laughed. "Yun's an auction. Dey hae een every week. Hit's mostly a load o' old bruk, but der's bargains tae be hed as weel. We can tak a look if du'd lik."

We decided to go along for a while. I might even find something to replace my rather decrepit fireside chair.

The auction room was an old hall. It looked a bit like a picture theatre that had seen better days. There was no shortage of the sort of furniture I had in mind. Whether it was for sale or not was another matter. A heterogeneous collection of lounge chairs and two-seaters were arranged in rows facing the front. The seats were occupied by elderly women, many wearing knitted hats and shawls over their shoulders. They all had their knitting with them and were chattering away like battery hens. It felt as though I had walked into a scene from the French Revolution. All it needed was Robespierre and the guillotine.

Presently the auctioneer arrived. Everyone quietened down. Then began the most extraordinary proceedings. There were about twenty or thirty cardboard cartons on the stage, all filled with odds and ends of kitchen utensils and bric-a-brac. I had noticed a few women poking amongst these when I had first come in. It soon became clear that the auctioning of these cartons was to be the main event of the afternoon.

The auctioneer obviously knew all the women by name and addressed himself to them exclusively. "Noo den, Bertha, dis looks a likely een fur dee," he would say, holding up a box and tantalisingly pulling out a couple of items.

The bidding was spirited, if rather difficult to follow. It seemed to consist of knit one, bid one. Purl to stay in or drop a stitch to retire. As Shetlanders are extremely fast knitters, however, it is difficult to tell when they are pulling the wool over your eyes.

When a box was knocked down to one of the women, an assistant would bring it to her and collect her money – seldom more than three pounds. The purchaser would immediately discard her knitting and begin to inspect her lucky dip. (One box seemed to be their limit.) It was pretty much as Young Bobby had intimated – a load of old bruk – books, magazines, pot and pans, glass vases, cutlery, oddments of wool, plastic bowls. Anything and everything that was worthless.

What followed was even more extraordinary. Each woman might select one or two items from her box, which she stuffed into her knitting bag or tucked away behind her in the folds of her shawl. The rest of the contents were repacked and the carton handed back to the assistant, presumably to be rearranged for the next week's auction.

I concluded the whole charade was a form of gambling for the women, and waited for someone to shout "Bingo!" when she discovered a real prize in her box. As the whole procedure seemed to take forever, we eventually tired of it and left empty-handed.

I learned later that the real auction took place in the evening, after a recess for tea. The old ladies only came to the afternoon session. I suppose at three pounds odd, it was cheap entertainment. And everyone got to keep their head.

Chapter Seven

Clare and Stephen came up for two weeks in August. When I heard they were coming I thought I would lay on a surprise meal for my darling sister. I asked Peerie Jessie where I might obtain some reestit mutton.

"Brenda Kellson maks da best reestit mutton in Bruntisdale," she said with a smirk. "Du best tak a run ower and see her. If du gengs noo du'll be in time to tak dee twal'oors wi' dem."

"Perish the thought," I said. "Maybe I'll just buy a couple of kippers instead."

"Na, na. Du'll hae to gie dy sister reestit mutton. Du's no feart for Brenda and Maggie is du?"

"Yes," I admitted.

"Ah weel," she said, taking pity on me. "Try Danny Sheltie. Sooth, ahint da kirk. I'll gie him a ring so he'll be lippenin' (expecting) dee."

Jessie no longer made any attempt to knap with me. She reckoned if I had planted kale in my backyard, I must be planning to stay a while, in which case I might as well learn to communicate properly. She had even begun to hint that it was time I found a wife and settled down.

"Du's spendin' too much time fishin' idda wrang burns, Stuart," was her candid opinion. No doubt she had short-listed several eligible females for my consideration. I had short-listed a couple myself, but I wasn't telling Peerie Jessie.

Danny Sheltie was another character in a village full of characters. He was a stocky fellow with a broad smiling face and curly blond hair.

He wore a blue serge cap, such as some taxi drivers seem to affect. He drove the school bus and was also the local councillor representing the district on the County Council in Lerwick.

Apparently he was a thorn in the side of the council, always attempting to divert funds to his pet themes which included a peat processing plant in the Bruntisdale scattald. He also had a plan to have cruise boats moor offshore and ferry tours to the Brat broch which he claimed was older and better than any other in Shetland.

As his scheme would land tourists at the foot of a cliff, which Danny proposed scaling by means of a zig-zag path blasted out of the rock – to say nothing of the amenities he planned on site, the whole idea was likely to cost a fortune. And that was just for the feasibility study!

Danny got his name from breeding ponies which he sold to eager buyers as far away as the Channel Islands. All his ponies were purebred Shetlands with sturdy legs and shaggy manes. They make ideal pets and are popular for beach rides at holiday camps throughout Britain.

I found Danny on his back under his school bus, draining the sump. He was wearing an extraordinary looking grey, hairy jumper that came down almost to his knees. It occurred to me the yarn might have been spun from horse hair. He looked like an English sheepdog that had rolled over to have its tummy rubbed. Even his tongue was sticking out the side of his mouth as he tried to get the thread started on the bung.

I had met Danny on a number of occasions so there was no need of introductions. Happily, we also dispensed with handshakes. Sump-oil is the very devil to get off. He was happy to sell me a piece of reestit mutton and took me to an airy room off his garage, where about fifteen hind quarters of mutton were hanging. The meat had darkened in the brine. It was quite shrivelled and looked unappetising.

Danny cut a sliver with his penknife and gave it to me to try. It was not unlike jerked beef I had eaten in Alaska, though rather gamey in flavour.

"Do we eat it raw?" I asked.

"You can, but most folks mak tattie soup on it. Suit yersel."

I thought the potatoes would take up some of the salt, so opted for the soup, letting it simmer at the back of the stove the greater part of the day, before serving it up to Clare and Stephen. It had been meant as a joke, but Clare claimed it was a gourmet treat. Stephen was less forthcoming. Personally I put Clare's fulsome praise down to the half-tumbler of Scotch she had had before dinner. I think I would recommend it as an essential adjunct to reestit mutton in any form.

Shetland sheep have a rather unusual diet which includes heather shoots and, of all things, seaweed. The sheep can be seen browsing the foreshore at low tide, sometimes wading into the sea for choice shoots. Consequently, the mutton has a distinctive flavour. It is something of an acquired taste, but once enjoyed, clover-fed lamb tastes bland by comparison. I must admit, when I left Shetland, it was one of the things I missed. I am referring to the fresh mutton however, not reestit. The reestit variety I am happy to leave to others.

During Clare and Stephen's visit we hiked to Brat broch. I had been saving the trip for such an occasion. It was late August and the weather was perfect. In fact, the entire fortnight they were with me, the sun shone every day. I had difficulty convincing them the weather was being especially kind. Clare said I was exaggerating when I claimed I more or less lived in wellington boots and a duffle coat.

"I swear it's true," I protested.

"Swear all you like, Stuart, but it's my belief you've gone soft. Only a wimp would wear a duffle coat in weather like this."

I gave up. After all, if the pictures in the tourist brochures were anything to go by, Shetland was a land of perpetual sunshine. Be that as it may, the hike to Brat broch was an unqualified success on a day of perfect weather.

We started at the mill (Stephen said there were similar ones in Israel), then we followed the burn inland for a mile or so before striking off towards the coast to be sure of not bypassing our objective. What breeze there was, was southerly, almost warm in our faces. The close-cropped grass was springy under our feet and full of daisies and crows-feet, with patches of thrift nearer the coast.

We found a hoody crow's nest in a cleft. It was a messy affair, similar to a black-back gull's, but with more sticks. Besides heather roots and tufts of wool, there were pieces of the ubiquitous orange twine which seemed to be a feature of every beach. No eggs or chicks of course, it was too late in the season.

I had expected the broch to be larger and in a better state of preservation after having heard Danny Sheltie rave about it. In fact it was rather disappointing as antiquities go. Not nearly as elaborate as the

Clickimin Broch in Lerwick, or as well preserved as the tower on the island of Mousa. Nevertheless the setting was magnificent. We voted it worth the visit for the view alone.

We ate our picnic lunch in the lee of the ruin, trying to imagine what it might have been like when it served as a fortress against marauding Vikings – if indeed it was built for that purpose. Apparently there are other schools of thought. It beats me how historians reach half the conclusions they do when they have so little to go on. (Presumably it will be easier for future generations to sift out information. They will simply visit a website rather than an archaeological site!)

It was highly unlikely Danny's hair-brained scheme would ever come to fruition. In any case I ardently hoped not. The attraction of the place was its isolation. Very few people bothered to go there. It was too far out of the way.

Places like Jarlshof and Clickimin – or Stonehenge, for that matter, are so overcrowded. The earth is beaten hard by teeming feet. Every stone has been touched till all are grimy with the sweat of a million hands. Cameras click at every turn. It might as well be Marble Arch or Piccadilly Circus for all the sense of antiquity you may hope to find.

At Brat broch I was able to marvel at the dry-stone walling, and contemplate the probability that some of the stones I patted had been touched by no other hands since the day they were placed with such precision by a Pictish stone-mason. I could walk to the centre of the fort, look up at the clear sky, listen to the cry of seabirds echoing from the cliffs below and fancy I heard more. Fancy I heard voices carried on the wind from centuries past. What was that line from the Up-Helly-A' song? ... *To wake the mighty memories of heroes that are dumb, The waves go rolling on.*

Clare was calling. "Stuart, are you going to stand there day-dreaming all day, or are we going to go and have a look at this loch you were talking about?"

I had planned the walk to include a visit to the head of Brat Geo then continue the short distance to Bratwater and thence back to the burn. I had especially wanted to check out the loch for its fishing potential. According to the contours of my map it was in a deep gully. And so it proved to be.

The loch was in a sort of crater. We were obliged to walk round the rim to where it fell away towards the gully out of which the burn ran. At all other points the sides were too steep. The only way to fish Bratwater would be by boat, launched from the western extremity. I said as much, though it was out of the question of course, owing to the isolation of the place.

"Perhaps Danny Sheltie could have one delivered by helicopter when he begins his feasibility study on the broch site," Clare suggested.

"Nice thought, Clare, but I don't think I'll hold my breath waiting," I said.

Stephen had gone on ahead of us and was sitting beside the burn with his head in his hands.

"He's not bored, is he?" I asked.

"Gracious no! He's probably letting his fertile imagination have free rein on a text for Sunday. By the look of him I'd say Elijah. He'll be expecting a raven to bring him bread any minute, I shouldn't wonder."

Clare picked up a flat stone and sent it skimming across the loch. "Nineteen!" she shouted with glee.

"I think we ought to go and rescue your husband," I countered, dodging the challenge. She knew I was hopeless at the game, having never managed better than around ten bounces.

"From what I've seen of ravens in these parts, they are all out for number one. 'Their ain fish guts for their ain sea maws', as they say. Anyway, Stephen's not preaching this Sunday."

"Yes he is. When we met that minister of yours in the shop the other day and he discovered Stephen is a rector, he said, 'Capital, capital. My people have never heard a Church of England sermon. You can be my guest and preach them one on Sunday.' Poor old Stephen was so taken aback he said he'd be delighted. Afterwards he asked me if I supposed there was any difference between a Church of England sermon and a Church of Scotland one."

"And what did you say?"

"I said, about half an hour, with the English out first for dinner."

"Yes, you have the right of it there," I laughed. "But you better tell him to be sure and quote from the King James Bible. The locals think all modern versions are not the true Word of God."

It was Clare's turn to laugh. "If I know my Stephen, he'll go all poetic after this day in the hills and give them something from Wordsworth."

"Not as a text, I hope," I said in some alarm. My few Sundays in Bruntisdale kirk, especially since the return of their own minister, had taught me that the liberal reforms advocated by the General Assembly in Edinburgh cut no ice here. The Bruntisdale congregation's idea of 'enlightenment' was best obtained in the darkness of the belly of Jonah's whale. Ignorance is bliss and bliss is what they sought. Who then, if asked for bliss, would give them a stone – or Wordsworth. Heaven forbid!

"Never fear," Clare reassured me. "The text will most probably be from Song of Solomon. Something bland and easily digestible. Stephen is a great believer in milk puddings."

"Well that's a relief," I said, and went to wake the evangelist from his reverie.

Chapter Eight

Needless to say, after Clare and Stephen returned south, the weather reverted to normal. The incentive to tramp the hills was consequently dampened, if you know what I mean. I settled to a routine of writing which at last began to show results.

The farm I had worked and lived on in New Zealand provided the background. It was now a matter of painting in the landscape and peopling it with real life characters. There had been no shortage of these in the district and now, as they began to reappear in my narrative, I was struck by how different they were to my present neighbours.

The farm encompassed over two thousand acres (more than the entire toun of Bruntisdale), and was one of several surrounding Arrowtown. Jagged snow-capped mountains formed a backdrop to the scene with nearer hills covered in brown tussocks of course grass providing the equivalent to the scattald for the fine-woolled merino sheep.

Each farm tended to be self-sufficient with very little social interaction between them. For the womenfolk in particular, this sometimes meant loneliness. Not that they had much time to think about it. Their days were always busy.

All the vehicles and the homestead had two-way radio. The women were always on call. In any given day they might be instructed to drive to town to collect spare parts for the tractors; vaccine for the calves; fencing staples; extra seed for planting. The list was endless.

They might have to drive the truck out to a remote water-hole, where a horseman with portable walkie-talkie had called in to say he had found a bogged steer which needed hauling out. One incident like this could end up wasting hours – though they were never wasted if the animal was saved. At other times first-aid might be required. A man fallen from a horse and concussed, or perhaps a lacerated arm caused by barbed wire snapping under tension. Or the task might be as mundane as taking lunch out to where the men were working, in order to save time on the job.

The men were never lonely, for they worked in the company of others and generally congregated at the pub in the evening. Women were not particularly welcome in the bar. Drinking was a man's thing. Occasionally the family might go for a 'counter meal' – steak and chips in the pub – but even then the wife could expect to drive the kids home on her own. Her husband would be dropped off by his mates later.

Sometimes I felt like speaking my mind about what I saw as unfair treatment of the womenfolk. I soon came to realise I would be wasting my breath. In most cases they entered the contract with their eyes open. They knew how it was and accepted it. They even appeared to enjoy it at times.

There was insufficient history in the place to have established much in the way of legend, such as made up the bulk of story-telling in Shetland that is. (The indigenous Maoris no doubt had their folklore but they did not mix much with the white settlers who employed me.) Instead, the New Zealanders embellished the ordinary events of yesterday and turned them into amusing tall tales.

A late session at the pub generally ended up as a sort of competition in which each tried to outdo the others, with the most outlandish story earning the teller the dubious right of shouting the last round of beers. A group of men drinking together like this was referred to as 'a school'. It was certainly an education. I repeat one of those late-night stories here, if only to show the improbability of the tale.

"Bill was a local bloke, renowned for his heavy drinking. He had set off for home on his bicycle after being chucked out of the pub at closing time. 'Home' was ten miles away, in the bush. It was a windy night. Bill was having great difficulty steering a straight path. Inevitably one of his wobbles coincided with a sudden gust of wind and the bike ended up in the ditch with a buckled front wheel. Bill dumped the wreck with a curse and continued on foot.

It started to rain. I should explain, when it rains in the South Island of New Zealand, cats and dogs is too mild an expression. Draught-horses might be nearer the mark. Rivers tend to break their banks within half-an-hour of onset.

Bill looked for shelter. He might be known locally as a 'soak', but enough was enough. He spied Harker's mailbox. Again I should explain. Country roadside mailboxes in New Zealand are designed to hold a week's supply of bread, a couple of cartons of beers, a drum or two of sheep drench and perhaps a sack of layer's pellets for hens. They have also been known to hold the mail. They are sometimes made out of recycled packing cases. The sort of thing that might have contained a deep-freeze or a short motor for a tractor. Forty-four-gallon drums lashed horizontally between a couple of posts are popular too. Painted on the side will be the farm RSD (roadside delivery) number.

RSD 38 was the Harker's mailbox. It was of the latter variety. Bill was a skinny runt. He reckoned he could squeeze in. He wiggled in head first and lay on his back with his feet sticking out. His boots got a bit soggy but that was nothing new. He was soon snoring gently, despite the rain kettle-drumming in his ears.

Bradley Harker had been out that night too. In his case it had been the hayshed down at the Richardson's place with Nora Richardson for cosy company. When Bradley rode up to his gate he was blissfully unaware of the rain. To him, the sky was starry. He dismounted the big stallion he was riding – seventeen-and-a-half hands – and hitched it to Bill's boots while he opened the gate.

Now it should not be supposed Bradley knew it was Bill's boots he was tying his horse to, but anyone who thought that night was starry, was hardly likely to pay too much attention to a hitching rail.

It took two hands and a certain amount of heaving to open the farm gate. Farm gates in New Zealand are like that. They sometimes fall off their hinges when they are halfway open. The Harker's did.

Meanwhile, Bradley's stallion was beginning to flare his nostrils and roll his eyes. He was a bit jumpy at the best of times and this was not the best of times. Something was spooking him. It might well have been the odour of Bill's socks.

Bill was having a problem too. He was allergic to horse-flesh, especially steaming horse-flesh. Bill sneezed. In the confined space, it sounded like a piston engine back-firing.

The stallion reared. Bill shot out of the drum like a cork from a ginger-beer bottle, flinging his arms about the horse's neck and hanging on grimly. It took remarkable dexterity and presence of mind on Bill's part to achieve this, but self-preservation was one of his strong points. His only strong point, some would say.

Next began a wild cross-country gallop with the stallion leaping fences and thundering through streams, all the while bucking and shaking its head in an attempt to rid itself of the limpet at its neck. The horse ran fifty miles that night, pulling up winded and broken on the outskirts of Queenstown. Bill slid to the ground and went in search of another mail-box. It was still raining.

When he came to in the morning, Bill was in the back of a school bus with a lot of strange kids shouting at the driver to come and see what they had found. Bill swore some joker had dumped him in a freight train. He distinctly remembered the click of the wheels and the train whistling in the tunnels. What he was unable to explain, was a letter in his back pocket, addressed to Bradley Harker."

As I said, the tales were unbelievable. The taller the better. Sending one another up was a favourite sport. It helped if you were thick-skinned and preferably not averse to colourful language of which the dominant shade was blue. These men were tough. They had to be to survive the quantities of beer they consumed. I am afraid I was no match for them.

Chapter Nine

It was September. The days were drawing in. There was a buzz of excitement in the village for a wedding was about to take place. The bride was a niece of Greta's. The bridegroom was a Lerwick boy with local connections. I was flattered to receive an invitation. Apparently everyone in Bruntisdale was expected to attend.

The service at the kirk turned out to be something of a fiasco. Greta was in charge of the seating, at least she took it upon herself to organise the ushers. She appointed her son Charlie to be responsible for the bride's side of the kirk, and his cousin Magnie, the bride's brother, was to seat the groom's side.

Part of the problem arose out of many guests being related to both sides. It was a common thing, by all accounts. Greta was said to be good at sorting it out. You needed the patience of Job and the wisdom of Solomon, because people 'took sides' as it were, in defiance of protocol. Nevertheless, it had to be done correctly. The old folks would be 'black affrontit' if a mistake was made. It all seemed a nonsense to me and I was pretty certain the happy couple could not have cared less. But that was beside the point.

Greta gave each of the boys a list, putting them on notice they would answer to her if they got it wrong. It would not have been a problem except that Freda Poulson, Peter's wife, who was another aunt of the bride, took exception to young Charlie's hand on her waist as he attempted to steer her in the right direction.

"Stop mauling me boy. I keen my ain gait. I'm no a fule!" Only she apparently did not 'keen her gait', for she sat two rows from the front on the wrong side.

Charlie sought counsel with his cousin, who thought they should tell the woman to move.

"You try telling her!" Charlie suggested. Magnie tried, half-heartedly it must be said, and got a flea in his ear.

"Go and bile your heid, Magnie. Du allus wis an interferin' idiot."

To make matters worse, Freda was an early arrival, thereby setting the pattern as it were. In her bright red hat she stood out like a sore thumb. Other relatives, seeing her, promptly went and joined her. Magnie, trying to usher the groom's relatives to the same side, got the brush off.

Charlie Green offered to "show him da toun o' Bruntisdale upside-doon," for getting in his way, and went to the wrong side.

By the time the bride arrived on her father's arm, Magnie was practically peeing himself. Charlie had done a bunk. Magnie's mother and aunt arrived at the same time. The first cuffed her son's ears and the other snatched the carefully prepared list from his hands, tore it to shreds and stuffed it down the front of his shirt. Thinking he might make amends, Magnie suggested his father swap sides with the bride, explaining it would "kinda square things up inside." He got another cuff for his pains.

When the organ struck up 'Here comes the bride', Magnie quietly closed the church doors from the outside and went in search of his cousin. He found him crouching in the car park.

"That's it then," Charlie said with a groan. "I'm off doon tae da pier tae throw mesel' in. Whin dy mither comes oot she'll et me."

Magnie offered an alternative. He had a bottle of rum in his car. There is nothing like a dram to put things in their proper perspective. (All this, I heard from Peter Poulson who thought it a huge joke.)

The reception went off rather more smoothly. The whole village was there. I must admit I thought it rather incongruous the groomsmen were all in kilts given the islanders' pride in their Norse heritage and the centuries old outlook that all they ever got from Scotland was 'bad meal and poor ministers'. It is amazing what a powerful influence fashion has on dress decisions. I wondered by what convoluted means the groom had settled on the Cameron tartan when his family name was Eunson, probably colour co-ordination with the bridesmaids' frocks.

I was seated next to Irene (about whom I will write more shortly). She had no family connections with the bridal party and had expressed her surprise at having been invited, given she was from another village. I saw Peerie Jessie's devious hand in this. She had been keeping a motherly eye on us for some months.

Irene commented on the changing ways of wedding receptions in recent years, noting the diminished community spirit that had once been the very soul of the event, and the competitiveness which had crept in as each tried to outdo the last in lavish trimmings and outlandish gimmicks.

Irene told me how it had been in her mother's day. All the local women were involved in preparing the reception, each being given responsibility for a setting of either six or twelve. The day before the wedding they came to the hall with their best tea-sets and their largest teapots, the latter suitably marked for identification with coloured string or wool round the handle.

The tables were long trestles covered with strong white paper, often the reverse side of cheap wallpaper. No electricity, of course, so Tilley lamps had to be primed and kept pumped up throughout the night. This was men's work, as was the carrying of water from the nearby well.

As extra water needed to be brought in for washing dishes and glasses, it was important the designated water-carriers be sober men. It was no time to lose a villager down the well, or have the water spilled by a drunker reveller on the way back.

The meal was always the same – cold mutton, bannocks (oven scones) and cakes. No lobster thermidor or baskets of exotic fruit, flown in from the Mediterranean à la our 1975 celebration.

Each table hostess received a three-pound bag of flour prior to the wedding in order to bake her bannocks. Several crofters killed and dressed choice young hogs (sheep). Others baked 'fancies' – small iced cakes. Each table had to have glass dishes of butter-balls, so butter pats were collected from those who made their own butter, and two or three women got together for a session. The rolled balls were kept in basins of cold water until required. No refrigeration!

A bus went round the village the day before, collecting the women for the various chores, and again on the wedding morning when platters of thinly sliced mutton, the fresh baked bannocks, fancy cakes, butter balls, jam, sugar and milk, had to be put on the tables.

A bar was set up in a side room, tended by two men chosen for their experience in managing this side of affairs. They also saw to the washing of glasses after each round of drinks.

Groups of five or six women took turns in the kitchen, some serving the main meal, others the supper.

Special items were borrowed for the bride's table. These included white linen tablecloths, cut glass decanters, even a particular fancy knife for cutting the cake. These things traditionally came from the same houses for every wedding.

When standing on the stage, where the bride's table was set, and looking down through the hall, an observer would see as many as fifty different china tea-sets, all with matching fancy folded serviettes, interspersed with vases of flowers. A colourful montage symbolising village unity.

Irene laughed when she recalled her mother's memory of wet nights, when all the women arrived at the hall in wellington boots with their dancing pumps in plastic bags under their arms and torches to light their way home.

"It could be a right steer in da cloakroom at four or five in da morning whin du tried tae fin dee buits," she said.

Late in September the school was closed for a day to allow the children to help with the tattie harvest. Young Bobby invited me to help with the 'lifting' on his rigs in exchange for "all the potatoes you need for winter!" It struck me as a good bargain.

There were two tractors in the village. Young Bobby owned one and the other belonged to Lowrie Petersen. In the course of the day they made the rounds of all the potato rigs, going from croft to croft with willing helpers running ahead to open gates. As the potatoes were ploughed to the surface, each family, with the help of neighbours, followed behind gathering the crop into sacks. Everyone pitched in, from the youngest to the oldest, with lots of chatter and laughter.

It was a back-breaking business. By the day's end I was exhausted, having helped on several crofts and done the rounds with the trailer when Bobby's tractor returned to cart the filled sacks to their various barns and outhouses. When I was finally dropped off at Westerfield with my sack of 'wages', I was glad of the huge bath and ample hot water supply to ease my aches and pains.

As I lay soaking, I reflected on the spontaneity of the whole affair. Like so much that took place in Bruntisdale, there appeared to be no particular leadership required. As far as I could determine, the whole business had been dealt with through some sort of telepathic mutual consent. A spell of fine weather and the sun westering in clear skies seemed to be sufficient to trigger the game-plan. All it needed was the season.' ... a time for everything, and a season for every activity under heaven'.

There was something immensely satisfying about this gentle order of things into which I had been drawn. I hoped they would always close the school for the tattie harvest, if only to teach the children the value of such co-operation. I remembered my own childhood when we lined up to hop under the whirling skipping rope:

One potato, two potato, three potato, four.
Five potato, six potato, seven potato, more.

Or:

All in together, this fine weather.

It suddenly made good sense.

As the days shortened towards the end of the year, I came to two decisions. The first was to extend my lease for a further six months in order to finish my project. The second was to put my fishing rod away for the winter and 'try anidder burn', as Peerie Jessie had advocated.

I had not come to Shetland in search of anything other than peace and quiet in which to write, however, I had found more. Her name was Irene ...

And now I must tell you about her.

When I thought of her (which I admit was frequently), I was put in mind of an Australian colonial ballad by C. J. Dennis, which I had learned at school. It was called 'The Intro', and began: 'Er name's Doreen ... ' going on in a rollicking fashion to describe the antics of a love-struck loon. Not poetry in the manner of Wordsworth, you understand.

The last lines are:

I carn't tell wot it is; but all I know
I've dropped me bundle – an' I'm glad it's so.

Fer when I come to think uv wot I've been ...
'Er name's Doreen.

It was not so much the 'wot I've been ... ' as the 'I've dropped me bundle – an' I'm glad it's so' that summed up how I felt. You might have to read the poem for yourself to get my drift. The point is, I had taken to substituting her name in the poem – 'Er name's Irene ... !

We had first met at the Johnsmas Foy. Regrettably, on that occasion I had not displayed the sort of behaviour likely to win respect, let alone anything deeper. As I have mentioned, the hip flasks passed my way rather too frequently, rendering the latter part of the night a blur.

Fortunately we hit it off early in the evening and Irene was apparently prepared to make allowances for the rest. She told me much later that I had offered to walk her home, but as 'home' was fourteen miles away and I was having difficulty making it to the door of the hall, she had declined. It appears my attempt at gallantry and my determination to escort her at any cost, so amused her that she fell in love with me there and then. It seemed an unlikely start to romance, yet the chemistry must have been there. From the moment I looked into her mischievous eyes I, too, was smitten.

In the morning she was the first thing I thought of. It was like a dash of cold water in my face – not a shock, more like exhilaration, with shivers down the spine for good measure. When I tried to analyse the feeling, I discovered it was a totally new experience for me. It made me think of the Arctic terns skimming and dipping across the water in search of those elusive flashes beneath the surface. For the first time in my life I had caught a glimpse of quicksilver and, like the terns, I had been given the perception to recognise it for what it was – a good catch.

I was delighted to find a note in my pocket with her name, address and telephone number, written in a bold hand. I cannot say I recall asking for it, in fact it is definitely not my style. I am much too reticent on first encounters.

When I eventually quizzed Irene on the matter, she looked me straight in the eye (a ploy of hers that was always reckoned to render me weak at the knees), and said, "Stuart, du's no suggesting I'd do a thing lik yun, is du?"

Her contrived childish innocence was laughable, as of course it was meant to be. What was I to say? "No," seemed to be what was called for. I said, "Yes."

"Of course du *asked* fur it," she protested. And I was left with the distinct sense of double entendre.

Perhaps I did ask, in which case the drink must have emboldened me and I would have to say the generosity of strangers proved most serendipitous. Even so, it took me a couple of weeks to work up the courage to ring her.

"Do you fancy a run in to Lerwick?" I asked.

"Suit yersel," she said. "Wir toun is no exactly on dy road du keens, but du can come by if du liks."

It wasn't exactly the response I was hoping for. It was to be a while before I could get her to say what *she* would like. Most frequently she would say, "Suit yersel," even when she knew fine I was desperate to discover what suited her.

For all that, it was a very satisfactory first outing. We lunched at the Lerwick Hotel – in style, you might say, and made the most of the long drive each way to find out as much as we could about one another.

I could give you an extremely accurate description of her, down to the number of freckles on her nose, the shape of the dimples in her cheeks (and her knees, for that matter), but beauty is in the eye of the beholder. Suffice to know, she could do extraordinary things to my respiratory rate simply by twinkling her eyes, or saying "Suit yersel' Stuart."

The first time she said "I love you" I kept demanding she say it again and again until she laughed and said, "I hate you," which sounded pretty much the same.

We made the most of the autumn days, hiking to remote corners of the scattald. The more remote the better; sitting by the side of a burn with cheese sandwich picnics; exploring caves at the ebb of the tide; slipping in piles of kelp and laughing at nothing.

We met frequently in Lerwick, Irene sometimes going by bus to rendezvous with me at Kveldsro Hotel (haddock in beer batter) or Da Noost (crumbed fillets), depending on our mood. We sat out on the Knab, watching the klondykers by the hour, till the cold wind drove us back to Da Street in search of a cup of coffee and a bun.

I was perversely secretive of our relationship as far as Bruntisdale folk were concerned, or thought I was. Irene's invitation to the September wedding, and her being seated next to me, proved how ineffectual I had been. I should have known better. When I realised which way the wind lay, it gave me the reason I needed to change my game-plan.

By the end of October I had extended the lease on the croft house for another six months and convinced Irene that I would never finish my book unless she came and cooked my meals. She didn't need much convincing. In consideration of this arrangement, I allowed her to share my bed, which is how I came to discover the configuration of the dimples in her knees. Some other configurations too.

As far as I can recall, I did no writing whatsoever during November. I do know it rained quite a lot as I distinctly remember the sound of it on the roof, which was very close to the head of the bed. Irene was a bit lax about the cooking during that month also. We began to get things a little more under control at the start of the festive season.

Clare and Stephen invited me south for Christmas but I declined. I said the book was at a critical stage and besides, I was enthralled by the 'merry dancers' – Shetland's aurora. I don't think Clare was fooled for one minute, but she kept her peace. I should have told her everything then and there, but I was not ready to share Irene with anyone. I was still at the stage of having to pinch myself to be sure I wasn't dreaming.

On fine nights we would lie in bed and count the number of stars we could see through the skylight. It was a game we played to determine how many children we would have. Sometimes there were less than a dozen. At other times they were countless.

On still nights we could hear the plaintive honking of whooper swans as they flew over us in skeins, making their way to the hill lochs. Once, in an enchanting moment, we saw a flock cross the patch of moonlight above our skylight.

"They mate for life, you know," I'd say, every time we heard them.

"What a nice thought," Irene would reply, wrapping herself around me and offering her lips to be kissed. When the moonlight made a square of light on the bedclothes, we would position ourselves in the centre of it and make love, then snuggle down again to count our children. We were childishly happy and contented.

One frosty night, when the aurora was rippling across the sky, we went outside to watch it. It was after midnight. Bitterly cold. We had the feather quilt wrapped around us, but shivered all the same. The frost crunched under our feet as we walked clear of the house to gain a good view.

The bands of colour, all the rainbow hues, were rushing up from the horizon on every side to a vanishing point above our heads. Merry Dancers indeed. At times we could hear a thin, eerie sound, as if someone was drawing a feather across the treble string of a violin. It was impossible to pinpoint the sound. Though I had heard tell of the phenomenon, it was my first experience of it.

"Da trow's 'll be dancin' idda hill tonight," Irene whispered, her eyes sparkling as they reflected the fiery display. In that moment she seemed strangely fragile and vulnerable. I gave an involuntary shudder and held her tightly to me, trying to will my heart to calm its wild beating. I loved her so much it hurt.

"If we stay here one minute longer, we'll turn to ice," I stuttered through chattering teeth.

"Du'll hae ta carry me. I canna win myself. My taes are frozen," she said with a giggle.

I was more than happy to oblige.

We turned the Rayburn to 'high' and opened the oven door. Irene made hot chocolate into which I tipped a sailor's ration of rum. It did wonders for our ardour. When it came to passion, the aurora had nothing on us.

Jessie and Bobby invited us over for New Year's Eve. I was for taking the car but Irene said, "Let's walk." There had been a light fall of snow and it glistened in the moonlight.

With one thing and another – mainly Peerie Jessie's teasing, and to some degree, Bobby's generosity with the bottle – Irene and I ended up officially engaged before midnight. Jessie said it was the best New Year's resolution she had ever heard.

We all strolled down to the end of the pier to see in the New Year. I am sure Bobby said there was some significance in our doing so, but for the life of me I cannot remember what it was. We were so cold when we got back to the house we needed a couple more drams to warm us, then Bobby got out the smelly fish van and ran us home.

It was the only socialising we did, apart from going to Lerwick regularly. The Kveldsro Hotel became our favourite eating place. The superbly cooked haddock in a crisp beer batter had the edge on all other choices of fish.

We did some 'pretend' shopping in Home Furnishings, arguing over pink or blue for the nursery and filling a cot with assorted stuffed toys, including an outrageously expensive pink elephant that had a ferocious looking expression which I thought might scare the baby.

On one visit to the town we went to the 'unction' – just for fun. Irene insisted on bidding for one of the mystery boxes, though she ended up keeping nothing except a pair of china egg-cups. At the price, we would have done better in Home Furnishings.

We were deliriously happy. Content to let life set its own agenda and pace. Unwilling to make any firm plans. Tomorrow was another day. Of course we were not blind to our feelings, and we readily expressed them. In fact, discovering one another's feelings was every bit as important and enchanting as discovering the sensual delights of touching. Saying "I love you" tends to open up whole new conversational channels and puts new meanings on everything else that is said. And like all lovers, when we ran out of things to say, we were not averse to murmuring sweet nothings.

Chapter Ten

On the 11th of January, in a night of lashing rain, Irene woke me around 3am. Her lovely eyes were dilated with pain and she was shivering uncontrollably even though her skin was burning with fever.

"It's me stomach," she groaned.

"Do you feel sick?" I asked.

She shook her head then closed her eyes as a spasm doubled her up. "Help me, Stuart," she whimpered.

I wrapped her in the quilt and carried her downstairs where I fired up the Rayburn. She sat curled in a foetal position in the old armchair, moaning every now and again. I felt powerless. I had nothing to give her apart from Panadol, which she refused. Brandy might have helped but I dared not risk it, not knowing what was causing the pain.

The nearest doctor was halfway to Lerwick. I swithered about going to the pierside phone and calling him, but decided it would be quicker to take Irene directly to the hospital. It would almost certainly be the doctor's recommendation in any case. I explained my plan, stroking her cheeks and squeezing her hands as I did so. Her hair was damp and clinging to her scalp, as if she had been out in the storm. Her eyes anxiously followed my every movement, though she said nothing.

Fortunately I was able to get her to the car without going outside as the garage adjoined the byre. I wound the passenger's seat back as far as it would go and laid her on it with pillows on either side and the quilt wrapped around her. (I had run the motor for five minutes to get the heater going before carrying her from the cosy kitchen.) Once on the road, I knew my trusty Audi would soon deliver adequate warmth.

It was no night to be out. The rain was coming at us in horizontal sheets so that the headlights barely picked out the nearest guide-post reflectors at the side of the road. I wanted to hurry but was forced to go at what seemed like a snail's pace. A misjudged corner would have us in the peat-bog with no hope of rescue for hours.

On such nights, sheep commonly huddled in the lee of road-cuttings, making an additional hazard to driving. My eyes ached from the strain of trying to penetrate the blackness, watching for tell-tale signs of movement at the extremity of the circle of light.

Every sort of demon seemed to lurk at the edge of that blackness too, all of them mocking me, reminding me how fragile life really is and how arrogant we are to assume our next breath is guaranteed. Instinctively I knew there was something seriously wrong. This was no ordinary gripe.

Beyond my occasional word of encouragement and reassurance, little was said on the journey. Irene lay still for the most part, moaning softly from time to time. I felt powerless to do anything and very frightened for her. I hoped there would be someone competent on duty at the hospital when we got there.

It was 7.15am before I saw the dim halo of Lerwick's first street lamp. It might have been the image of Christ, for the sense of relief it gave me. The Gilbert Bain Hospital was now only minutes away. Surely everything would be okay now.

But it wasn't. After the urgency of the journey, the stress and worry, things at the hospital seemed to go into slow motion. In the car I had been fully in control (if you could call it that), gripping the steering wheel until my knuckles turned white, clenching my teeth, counting off the miles, willing Lerwick ever nearer. Now I was limp and useless. Going nowhere. Doing nothing.

Nor did anyone seem to subscribe to the sense of emergency which I felt ought to attend the situation. There was no drama. More importantly, no-one came forward to demonstrate the degree of competence I was looking for, though I must admit I was in no position to judge. Irene had been wheeled away and everything had gone quiet. I would have felt better if people were rushing about.

Surely there ought to be hurried consultations in the corridors. Phones should be ringing incessantly. The place was like a morgue ... No! Not a morgue. Perish the thought. A church, maybe.

Someone brought be a cup of lukewarm tea with too much milk in it. I began to worry. I began the 'what ifs?'. Up to now I had been too busy to think, too busy controlling the car, concentrating on the job in hand. Now it was up to others. I was superfluous, impotent, terrified. I wanted to ask questions but there was no-one to ask.

The clock on the wall had stopped at 3.15. Hadn't Irene wakened me around then? Was that significant? A poster asked me if I was immunised against diphtheria. I wasn't sure. My mother would probably know. No she wouldn't. My mother never knew anything concerning my wellbeing. I wondered if the clock was electric or if it needed a battery.

Daylight came. If you could call it daylight. Murky grey instead of black. A few indistinguishable dreary buildings beyond the window. Cold, leaden sky. I thought the blackness preferable. At least there had been a touch of warmth in the streetlamp halos. There were puddles in the car park where the asphalt had broken.

Some time later a doctor came and spoke to me. He wore a stethoscope round his neck like a badge of office. I thought it pretentious. I don't remember much of what he said. I think I was in some kind of delayed shock. I felt numb. There was some reference to no planes flying to Aberdeen because of the weather, and waiting for the surgeon. Surely they weren't flying a surgeon up from Aberdeen! I might have asked, only the information took a while to sink in. By then, he'd gone.

Much later a nurse came by and asked if I would like something to eat. I said, "No thanks," ... at least I think I did. She brought me tea and sandwiches anyway. Some sort of meat paste. I couldn't eat them. I must have dozed after that.

Someone was shaking me. A man in a white coat. No stethoscope. A real doctor? It was dark outside. The streetlights were casting their halos once more.

"What's happening?" (Was that my voice? A sort of squeak, like a frightened rabbit.)

"We have operated and removed the obstruction," he said.

Obstruction?

(In the following days it was variously referred to as a 'growth' or a 'tumour' – I never did establish the truth of it.)

The doctor said I could go and see Irene for a couple of minutes.

When I saw her, she seemed to have already gone from me. She was hooked up to two drips. One was labelled 'Addictive'. Morphine, I presumed. There was a tube in her neck and another in the back of her right hand. There didn't seem to be very much of her available to touch.

I lightly kissed her cheek. It felt cold and clammy, not the warm, vibrant cheek I knew. The one with the quirky dimple that came and went with her smile. She was unaware of my presence. Or was she? Who could say?

"I'm sorry, you must leave now," the nurse whispered.

I had only just got there.

After that I lost track of things. I forgot where I had parked the car. I forgot what day it was. I forgot to eat. I pretty much forgot everything except my need to get Irene back home safe and well.

The days ran into one another. Sometimes I sat for hours watching the intravenous drip. The shrinking bag which was supposedly delivering sustenance to Irene, seemed rather to symbolise the way in which the life was draining from her. I tried to will her to fight but she gave no sign of doing so.

A parade of nurses came and went with the changing shifts, each taking turns to hourly measure the vital signs – pulse, blood-pressure, temperature – then faithfully charting everything for others to draw conclusions. What conclusions? I felt they were merely going through the motions. It seemed so routinely detached from the vital woman I loved.

I idly wondered if my Irene was already somewhere else, perhaps going through one of those 'out-of-body experiences' people talk about. Floating up near the ceiling looking down at me. In two minds about whether to come back or head on down the tunnels toward eternal light.

Perhaps if we had discussed the matter beforehand, we would each know what the other thought and act accordingly. But you are never prepared for something like this, are you? It takes you by surprise. Nor are there any ground rules for dealing with it. None I am aware of, at least. Perhaps someone should write a book. Come to think of it, didn't Dr Elizabeth Kubler-Ross write something noteworthy on death and dying? Trouble is, it is not the sort of thing you go looking for until it is too late.

I booked a room at the Lerwick Hotel (a short walk down the road), though I scarcely spent any time there. I no sooner got there than I felt the urge to hurry back to the hospital. What if Irene needed me at the precise moment I was taking a shower or a quick nap in my comfortable room?

Whenever I returned to sit with her, I could see she was slipping away from me. She never woke sufficiently to communicate with me, though I thought she squeezed my hand a couple of times. Or was it wishful thinking?

Irene clung precariously to life for six days, which included a second operation to try and combat peritonitis. The doctors were deliberately vague about her chances, though I guessed from their doublespeak they held little hope. In the end she died quietly in her drug-induced sleep. I was with her, yet unaware she was no longer with me.

Someone put an arm around my shoulder and gently but firmly drew me out of the room.

"You should try and get some sleep," I was advised. "There is nothing more you can do here."

I could say I had come to expect Irene's death, but I hadn't. Not really. You never do expect it. You never give up hope. At least I didn't. I defiantly went on planning our future together, as if by doing so I could make it happen.

Once I got over the initial shock, I railed against God. By what right had He taken her from me? He had all the angels He needed. I cursed Him. I wished Him in hell. (Not very original, I admit.) I called Him a coward for hiding behind His rain-sodden clouds and not confronting me.

Eventually I gave up and begged for understanding. Even in that, I was denied. I was granted numbness, which I had not asked for, but supposed was better than nothing. Out of the numbness came sleep.

Two days after she died, I walked past the town hall and heard the clock strike the hour. It put me in mind of a German proverb father used to quote:

When a man is happy he does not hear the clock strike.

I imagined I would always hear it from then on.

I became acutely aware of the fragility of life. In the park nearby, snowdrops would be stirring to life, preparing to thrust up through the late snows of March. But there were no guarantees. Some freak of nature might thwart the plan. Or man could intervene. It wouldn't be the first time. Councils are forever digging holes in the most unlikely places. The snowdrop bulbs might be tossed aside to die.

Nothing is assured, I told myself. Not any more. All of life is a mystery. Geese may walk over our graves. Who has not felt it was so at one time or another? Nor can we do anything about it. We are at the hand of fate – or God, if you will.

The next day, on the way home, I saw the white weasel dancing in the snow. I stopped the car to watch it. If it was aware of my presence it was unperturbed. In fact, it seemed to be performing especially for me, dancing on a large slab of rock as though it were a stage. A tantalising poetry of motion. Weaving, flowing, full of life, soft and warm. Everything else was rigid and bleak and cold. I thought of the line of a Christmas carol:

Earth as hard as iron, water like a stone.

And in the midst of it, this exquisite little creature.

I was kept spell-bound for several minutes. Enthralled. Apart from myself the weasel was the only life in a lifeless landscape. I came to believe it was the spirit of Irene, released into those barren hills to bring them perpetual joy and hope. The sense of her presence was so real I could scarcely bear it. I heard her voice again, from the night of the aurora: "Da trow's 'll be dancin' idda hill tonight."

Irene had told me she believed in the trows. If you believe in something, then anything is possible within that belief. If I must relinquish Irene, then it would be to the trows, whose mischief and laughter and merry dance would keep her forever young and joyful.

Chapter Eleven

When I returned to Bruntisdale I walked to the end of the pier and contemplated jumping off. It would have been futile. I am much too strong a swimmer. Instead, I went home to my empty croft house where I moved the bed so I no longer had a view through the skylight. I could not bear to see the stars.

Towards the end of the week they brought her body back in an oak casket to lie a night at the front of the church. I sat a while with her in the darkening, speaking silently about the love we had shared – the love we would always share. What I said made little sense but it made me feel better.

I didn't have much to do with the funeral. Her relatives took care of things, claiming her back for themselves at the end. I did one good thing, however. I persuaded Peerie Jessie to ask the womenfolk to attend the funeral. I have no idea what the break with tradition meant to them, but they all came.

It made it harder and easier for me. Easier, because their warm-hearted embraces were so much more comforting than the formal handshakes of the men. And at the same time harder, because I lost control. But I knew it was right. Right to cry, and right for others around me to cry too.

I telephoned Clare after that. She caught the first plane up and gently chided me for not having told her sooner. As usual she was right. It would have been good for Clare and Irene to have met. It would have helped me too.

Clare stayed a few days, trying to persuade me to go back with her. I said I had to finish the book first. Irene had read my work and thought it 'splendid'.

"You must finish it, Stuart," she had urged.

She had even gone so far as to threaten to leave me if I didn't get on with it. When I remembered the remark I was appalled to realise that that was what she had done.

Clare wanted to read the manuscript but I said no, she could buy the finished product. Instinctively I knew Clare would have to express her opinion. However much she might want to encourage me, she would be unable to be less than frank. I was not prepared for my sister's frank opinion – not yet, anyway.

It was beyond Irene to give a critical assessment. No matter how bad a writer I might be, Irene would lavish praise on my work. In my vulnerable state I knew I could only complete the book in the strength of Irene's loving encouragement.

Clare conceded defeat on all fronts and returned to Eyemouth. Her departure was the catalyst I needed. Even as I continued to mourn Irene's death, I found escape in the otherness of my book. Even when I was not actually typing the text, my mind was composing phrases, shading in background or sharpening focus.

Mostly I used the writing as a ploy to keep away the pain of my loss. Mostly it worked, but sometimes it triggered a memory which brought the emptiness flooding in. Then I would have to go for a walk. Go somewhere that belonged to the time before Irene, in a desperate attempt to keep her at arm's length. Not because I wanted to, but because any nearer association overwhelmed me.

Eventually I was able to let her back in. Welcome her in fact. I could bear to recall her touch, her quirky dimples, her mischievous eyes, her funny remarks. All of that. And I could smile again. It was a good feeling, or at least as good as it could get I supposed.

There was a subtle change in my relationship with the village folk. Before, they had been warm and friendly, yet never taking liberties. Now they took me to their hearts. Maggie Petersen, in particular, took it upon herself to nurture me. She came up to the house most days.

"Noo then, Stuart," she'd say, throwing her arms around me while we both had a good cry. Then I would make a cup of tea. We would make inconsequential small-talk for a while, comfortable in one another's company. Never in a hurry. Speaking about the weather (always a safe subject) or the eternal round of crofting work.

Eventually Maggie would rise.

"So, my dear, I'll be goin' noo." And she would lay a hand against my cheek in a kind of benediction, sighing as her eyes filled with tears once more.

As time passed I found myself consoling her more than she consoled me. It seemed as if my loss had reopened Maggie's own wounds or that she had taken on my grief and made it her own. Later on I came to realise the extent to which she had contributed to my healing.

There was a similar reaction from many others. Whenever I went into the shop Peerie Jessie would say, "Noo then, Stuart, this is you," as if she was expecting another.

Any other shopper with their back to me, was thus given warning to leave off whatever frivolous conversation had been going on and assume a suitably lugubrious expression. It was obviously going to be up to me to declare an end to the state of mourning, else the entire village was in danger of being swamped by the perpetual outpouring of sadness.

The weather had taken up towards the end of January. A few calm days with a blink of sun. Everyone was looking forward to Up-Helly-A', with members of the Jarl's squad showing off the beards they had so assiduously grown over the winter months. It was an established tradition that the Viking squad who manned the galley ship, must all be suitably hirsute. Presumably they considered it added to the villainous appearance they sought to portray.

I did not attend the festival in Lerwick but I put in an appearance at the local event, accepting the passed hip flasks which helped bolster my failing spirits. Though I went home with a headache, it marked the turning of a corner for me.

The next day I tied a few flies and thought about one or two likely spots I might visit if the rain held off long enough to make the countryside traversable in anything other than thigh boots. I might even take Peter's advice and try the end of the pier. Second thoughts counselled otherwise. I had conflicting emotions about the end of the pier. Somewhere beyond the binoculars might be better.

The weather gods conspired to keep me indoors much of the time, so that my book continued to take shape. I had taken to thinking of it as a 'book'. I designed covers. I dreamt up glowing literary critiques for the flyleaf. I even began seeing my name in larger letters than the title, like some of the popular writers you see in airport bookstalls. Ridiculous stuff I know, considering the insurmountable odds I faced.

I was perfectly well aware that infinitely better writers than I could ever hope to be, had papered their walls with rejection slips. What did I care? I was escaping into another world. When it ended, as it must soon, I would come down off my cloud and go back to breeding Suffolk sheep, or whatever. For the time being it was the balm I needed.

I put the finishing touches to the manuscript towards the end of April then treated myself to a last couple of weeks serious fishing, visiting all the outlying lochs and even joining Peter at the end of the pier. He was right about sitting 'peaceable on a rock'. The fish did not disturb us at all.

Then it was time to go. I went to Leask's in Lerwick and booked my flight south for the 15th of May. It would be almost a year since my arrival. Four seasons and the full emotional gambit. There was still a dull ache in my heart, but contrary to my expectations, I seldom heard the strike of the clock.

I took flowers to Irene's grave one last time, sitting for a while beside her as I reflected on what might have been. She had fancied the idea of being lady of the manor one day, joking about how many servants she would need. We hadn't really talked much about the future, content to live for the present. Now it seemed as well it had been so. It was bad enough to lose Irene without losing impossible dreams as well.

I had given some thought to making an offer on the croft house with a view to using it for holidays from time to time. It would have made sense to keep a Shetland base if Irene was going to become a permanent part of my life. Now, however, it seemed more likely I would close the door on this chapter of my life once I left. For all that I had grown to love the place and the people, I could not imagine myself staying or coming back without Irene. I was aware my feelings might change with the passing of time, but for the time being I had booked a one-way ticket south.

I dared myself to count the stars through the skylight one last time, but when it came to it I found I couldn't. What would be the point? Better to turn the key in the lock. If I had a record of Edith Piaff singing 'No Regrets', now would have been the time to play it.

I said my goodbyes to everyone, going from house to house as the seamen used to do when they went off to the whaling. It was an emotional time. Everyone had a gift for me. Danny Burnside had fashioned a miniature tushkar.

"Du's no a real Shetlander till du cuts dee ain paets," he said.

"I'll cast up twartree whin I gang oot troo da hill," I promised, showing off my mastery of the dialect.

And I did, silly as it was.

Maggie had knitted me yet another jumper, belittling it in her usual manner, though she knew fine how much it pleased me to receive it. I might have been the son she lost, for the amount of loving kindness she lavished on me.

Lowrie let his wife do most of the talking as usual, smiling and nodding by turn to assure me he was in accord with all she said. When he shook hands with me at the door, he passed me a slip of paper. I raised my eyebrows.

"Just a wee word from the Guid Man hissel," he murmured and I saw it was a biblical text he had given me: 2 Thessalonians 3:16.

When I looked it up later, it confirmed what I had always known. With shepherds like Lowrie in the world, it is little wonder Christ used the vocation as His preferred analogy when referring to His own calling.

Young Bobby gave me a bottle of Glenfiddich single malt.

"Du'll mind wis whin du taks a dram?" Peerie Jessie admonished, brushing away a tear.

"Du keens I will!" I replied, my own tears threatening to spill over. I think my leave-taking from Bobby and Jessie was the hardest.

When I stopped beside Old Bobby to shake his hand in farewell, he patted the bench beside him as usual.

"Dip dee doon a start, boy, I hae somethin' fur dee."

He took from his pocket the piece of scrimshaw I had so much admired, the one with the boy and the old man on the quayside. When I protested, he stuffed it in my jacket pocket.

"It's nothin'," he said, then added with a sly wink, "Du'll meybe get a bob or two fur it in Edinboro, whin du's hard up."

I drove out of Bruntisdale in the early morning before anyone was likely to be up, not sure of being able to cope with any last minute farewells. I might have known better. I met Tom Renwick heading down to his trawler. He stopped his car in the middle of the road, effectively blocking my escape.

"Whit's dis, then?" he said, strolling across to the side of my car. "Sneakin' aff afore sun-up. Tut, tut."

I gave a wry smile.

He shook my hand.

"Ah weel, du meybe hes da right o' it, Stuart. Some o' wis 'id as like try and keep dee at da last. Dir no that many comes in ower da grid yonder that we tak all that much fancy tae ... least none that can mak a proper job of shearin' a sheep, that is. Du'll be sorely missed."

We both laughed.

"You could take trawl a shade further south now and again," I suggested.

He gave me a quizzical look.

"You know! Drop me off a nice box of North Bank's haddock in Eyemouth."

"Oh, that. Yus, yus, I'll do that right enough." And he clapped me on the shoulder.

"Take care of deesel, Stuart."

"You too, Tom."

And so I made my escape.

I left the car with Leask's, having arranged with them to sell it for me. A year of salt-laden wind in the isles made it less than prudent to take it back south. In any case, I was due to update the model.

As the plane banked out over Jarlshof (that much photographed piece of antiquity at the end of the runway), I had a glimpse of Sumburgh lighthouse and fancied I could see tammie norries sitting at the entrances to their burrows. A couple of trawlers were heading up to Lerwick in a calm sea after a night's fishing east of Fair Isle. 'Life goes on', seemed to be the message.

My manuscript was tucked in a zip file in the locker above my head. Was it worth the effort? Well, that remained to be seen. Now that it was finished it was no longer an issue. What counted was that I had given a big piece of my heart to a place and its people. I might have to go back and reclaim it one day.

I took Old Bobby's scrimshaw from my pocket, turning it over and over in the palm of my hand, feeling the smooth patina of the ivory and the fine etching. I studied the workmanship. The entire picture would be virtually invisible until Bobby ran the Indian ink over it and rubbed it in. Thinking about it, it seemed to me to be a lesson in life, the darker moments giving everything a necessary perspective. Rather in the way the etched lines on Old Bobby's face revealed the hardships he had endured. Indeed, in exploring hidden depths within myself over the past year, I had no doubt etched a line or two into my own face. Might others now read volumes in what they saw?

Perhaps I had been the boy in the picture, desperate to get my hands on the telescope and get a glimpse of distant horizons. Now I must learn from the older man and be at peace. Shetland and the Shetlanders had taught me much about patience and peace; about gentle humour and beauty; but most of all I had learned the value of genuine friendship and love.

The jolt of the undercarriage locking down brought me from my reverie. I glanced out the window to see a shining river. It was easily identified as the Forth by the bridge that spanned it. We would be landing at Edinburgh airport within seconds.